Praise for Heather Blanton

"Heather Blanton infuses her stories with immense grace and dignity."

—LINDA BRODAY, *NEW YORK TIMES* BESTSELLING AUTHOR

"Heather Blanton is blessed with a natural storytelling ability, an 'old soul' wisdom, and wide expansive heart."

—MARK RICHARD, EXECUTIVE PRODUCER OF AMC'S *HELL ON WHEELS*

"Fans of Louis L'Amour and Francine Rivers will find Blanton's stories even more enthralling. With wit, a clear author's voice, and storytelling chops that rival the best—you'll have found your new favorite storyteller!"

—CARRIE FANCETT PAGELS, AWARD-WINNING AUTHOR

"Masterful at gritty fiction that points to the ultimate Creator, Heather will become one of your favorite Christian fiction authors."

—KARI TRUMBO, *USA TODAY* BESTSELLING AUTHOR

Daughter of Defiance

Also by Heather Blanton

Grace Be a Lady

Daughter of Defiance

ROMANCE IN THE ROCKIES
BOOK FOUR

HEATHER BLANTON

Author's Note

Dear Reader,

Jesus was the greatest storyteller of all time. As a writer, I pray my words will be a fraction as powerful as His. His ability to change hearts and minds with a simple story is fascinating to me. Hence, the model for my Defiance tales.

Readers who have been with me for a while now know that the town of Defiance is analogous to our culture. My characters, like you and I, do not live in bubbles. They face challenges to their faith every day. Sometimes they make the Lord proud. Sometimes they don't. Sound familiar?

The theme of *A Promise in Defiance* is that our choices have consequences...but there is always grace. We are poor, flawed vessels for delivering His truth to a dark world. He never expected us to be diamonds. Lumps of coal are fine with Him. Who we are doesn't change one iota Who HE is, though. He is the very Creator of the universe. The God Who loves us so much, He sent His Son to die for us...even while knowing that sacrifice would not make us perfect, but would make us something better: redeemed!

My readers know I love to research, and there is a ton of actual historical information in my stories. My character Delilah Goodnight is based on the real Mary Hastings, a Barbary Coast madam. Such a debauched person, I actually held back a little in creating Delilah. In other words, she isn't as bad as she could have been!

A big hat-tip to the Wyoming newspaper archives. I could have stayed lost in all those articles covering the Indian problem, Red Light Abatement Laws, and so much more! A real step back in time.

Finally, I would like to specifically thank Barbara Barton for her wonderful book *Pistol Packin' Preachers: Circuit Riders of Texas*. These frontier preachers faced Indians and outlaws to deliver the Gospel over hundreds of miles of wild terrain. The insight I gleaned from them was invaluable to developing my character of Logan Tillane.

Thank you for journeying along with me as Charles and Naomi and all the family once more try to tame Defiance!

God bless, y'all!

Heather

Preface

Can Jesus redeem anyone? The simple point of this story is yes. From the prodigal son to the apostle who denied Him three times, God offered mercy, redemption, and a fresh start. If you've been forgiven, then you know you have much to be thankful for, and this season probably means a lot to you.

If you're still struggling, still running, still rebelling, I encourage you to consider God loves you—no matter what.

He loves you with a fierce passion. He loves you just the way you are.

But He refuses to leave you that way.

The quality of mercy is not strained.
    It droppeth as the gentle rain from heaven
    Upon the place beneath. It is twice blest:
    It blesseth him that gives and him that takes.
    'Tis mightiest in the mightiest, it becomes
    The thronèd monarch better than his crown.
    His scepter shows the force of temporal power,
    The attribute to awe and majesty
    Wherein doth sit the dread and fear of kings,
    But mercy is above this sceptered sway.
    It is enthronèd in the hearts of kings,
    It is an attribute to God Himself.

—PORTIA, IN WILLIAM
SHAKESPEARE, *THE MERCHANT OF
VENICE*

Daughter of Defiance

Prologue

"MURDER AIN'T anything she should get away with."

The campfire popped and crackled, punctuating Oscar's defiant tone. The two other men with him—Lawrence and Charlie—nodded, the flames painting all three in an uneasy mix of light and midnight shadows.

"And she won't," Oscar continued, waving his bottle. "I ain't backing off now."

"What if she ain't there?" Charlie asked as he languidly settled on his bedroll. "If she ain't, I'm probably done following you two around." He sounded bored and a little sleepy. "This has been a long row to hoe."

"Then be done," Oscar spat, sloshing a little whiskey in the fire. It flared ferociously, the light illuminating the trio for an instant. He contritely pulled the bottle closer to his chest and spoke more calmly. "We don't need you. You invited yourself along anyhow."

"True, I did. I was curious to see if you two could find her. But this road is gettin' long. Summer is comin' to an end."

"It ain't over yet," Lawrence said, the certainty in his gravelly voice a harbinger of death. "Long as Jamie lies at the bottom of that mine, we'll keep looking."

"Well, I *will* say," Charlie began as he turned his back to his comrades and folded his arms for warmth, "If you two do find Delilah, I sure wouldn't want to be in her shoes."

One

VICTORIA PATTERSON STARED at the saloon's batwings and took a deep breath. It did nothing to still the butterflies in her stomach or restore the strength to her wobbly legs. A knot formed in her throat and she swallowed it down.

Victoria was terrified to see her mother again after all these years...and, yet, *desperate* to see her.

She pinched away sweat from her upper lip with a gloved hand and looked down at her simple, blue cotton dress. Brushing her fingers over the paisley patterns at her stomach, she smiled bitterly. She was no longer the satin-draped, diamond-encrusted, rouged-up Delilah Goodnight. The party was over.

Used up, empty, and broken, she had returned to Dodge City. Would her mother care to see the prodigal return? Victoria squeezed her eyes shut and felt around in the mental darkness for a shred of courage.

I have to go in there.

But what if she knows about me? All that I've done? What happened in Defiance? She'll hate me.

And if she does, you can just keep right on moving east.

The same two warring voices in her head that had been arguing since leaving Colorado. But Victoria had to know. Had to see if there was any hope for love...for sanctuary...for peace.

She raised her hand to push the batwing out of the way but paused when she heard humming. Coming from the alley beside the saloon. Victoria knew her mother's voice instantly, even after all this time.

Shocked that she had to fight back a sob, she drifted unsteadily over to the edge of the porch and peered down the alley. Eleanor Patterson, a heavy-set woman with her mostly-gray and brown hair pulled into a bun, stood on the stoop, shaking out a rug. She was older and bent a little, most likely from work like this. Still humming, she draped the mat over the rail, went inside, and returned a moment later with another. Snapping it back and forth, she paused quickly to mop her brow with a corner of her apron.

Victoria's heart was firmly lodged in her throat. How many years? Fifteen? All that time, thinking her mother had sent her to a house of prostitution on purpose. The results of the action —well-intentioned or not—were still echoing in the universe.

If only things had turned out differently...

Victoria pushed away from the darkness of the thought and forced her legs to move. She descended the steps to the alley as if she were walking on glass. She approached Eleanor slowly, silently, came to within a few yards, and stopped.

Finally, the woman looked up. A bland curiosity glimmered in her eyes, then slowly, something else dawned there and her face went slack. She moved her mouth, but no sound came out.

Her shock freed Victoria to speak. "Momma, it's me. Victoria. I'm back."

Eleanor remained incapable of speech for another moment,

but finally, tears sprang to her eyes and the rug slid from her hand. "Victoria?" she whispered hoarsely.

Victoria gave up her own fight and let the tears flood her eyes and spill down her cheeks. "Yes." It came out as a jagged croak.

Eleanor shook her head as if finally realizing the moment's import and ran down from the stoop. She flung herself at Victoria and hugged her daughter with a desperate, vice-like grip, her sobs shaking both their bodies. Aware this affection probably wouldn't last—not once Victoria told her mother her story—she still gave in to the moment. She returned the hug with the desperation of a human starved for affection, kindness, and, most of all, love.

"Oh, Momma, I have missed you so much."

The two women held each other for several minutes until Eleanor finally backed away, sniffling. Her ruddy cheeks were slick with tears. "Oh, Victoria." Hazel eyes glistening, she patted Victoria's cheek. "My daughter, my daughter. I feared I'd never see you again, but I knew you were alive. I knew it."

"Momma..." Victoria wiped one of her mother's cheeks. "I'm alive. I'm back. But I have so much to tell you and—" her voice broke and her own tears returned. "And most of it's awful about me."

Eleanor's expression of weepy joy changed. Her round, slightly-weathered face softened with love and mercy. She tilted her head and took her daughter's hand. "Oh, baby girl, it makes no difference. You're home. That's what matters to me."

Victoria watched her mother prepare a simple breakfast of eggs and bacon. The cramped quarters of the little kitchen in the back of the saloon barely gave the woman enough room to shuffle about. After setting two plates of fried eggs on the table, Eleanor poured them each some coffee and finally sat. Victoria had drifted, staring into the black, steaming cup, but she could feel her mother's frank stare like a hand on her shoulder.

Where to start? She supposed at the beginning. Fifteen years ago. "When you put me on the stage to Stillwater that day, where did you think you were sending me?"

"You know. I had a job for you at the Stillwater Inn. Cleaning rooms. I told you I did that to get you out of here, away from some of the things I was doing, get you around decent people. Away from…"

"Away from Logan." Victoria laughed softly, bitterly. "You sent me to a brothel."

The blood drained from Eleanor's face, her expression changed to a mask of horror and pain. "What?"

"It was a bordello. The man—Sam Collins—he was a pimp. I thought you sold me. He said you sold me."

Eleanor's ample bosom rose and fell like it belonged to a winded horse. Her chin trembled. Right before Victoria's eyes, the woman seemed to age a decade. "God as my witness, I didn't know," she whispered. "I would never have done that. I only wanted to keep you away—I mean, give you something better." Her words came in a rush. "I thought I could trust him. He never—he never came to see me for that. He said he had a wife and family…no wonder you never wrote—" Visibly shaken, Eleanor sagged in her chair.

Victoria didn't exactly have pity for her mother, but at least the hate she'd harbored for the woman all this time was gone. "It doesn't matter now, Momma."

Eleanor pressed a hand to her mouth. Her eyes flooded again. "I just wanted you safe. He said it was a nice hotel. There would be opportunities for you—"

Victoria reached across the table and took her mother's hand. "All water under the bridge now. No matter what—" a knot drew tight again in her throat and she had to fight past it. "No matter what you did or thought you did, I made the decisions from there. Horrible ones."

Eleanor seemed to sense her daughter's desperation and changed the grip, taking Victoria's hand in hers. "Tell me." She nodded, clearing the way. "Get it said. Whatever it is."

Victoria couldn't stop the fresh tears. They came suddenly in a scalding flood. "I don't want to," she said, the words tangled in a sob. "I'm afraid you'll hate me and make me leave." Oh, how had she come to this sniveling, disheveled mess? The old Victoria had never cried. Because she'd never cared about anything but power. Shame heated her cheeks.

"My darling daughter, I will never make you leave again." Eleanor squeezed Victoria's hand tighter, almost desperately. "I'll never lose you again, Victoria. No matter what you've done, no matter where you've been, I love you. And I've been waiting right here for you all these years."

That sounded just like something Logan would have said about God. The pain of missing the man twisting in her heart, Victoria lowered her head to the table, hid her face in the crook of her elbow, and tried to get the debilitating, life-sucking grief under some kind of control. Her auburn curls, once piled high and pinned with gem-studded jewelry, spilled messily around her. "I changed my name. You probably heard it and never knew it was me."

"What did you change it to?"

She hesitated but knew delay was pointless. "Delilah Goodnight." Her mother's gasp was soft, barely audible, but Victoria heard it just the same. What was worse? Her reputation as a decadent, no-holds-barred madam, or the devastation she'd wreaked in Defiance? Resigned to facing the music, she sat back up.

Eleanor's eyes were wide with surprise and revulsion. The last vestige of hope for anything good in Victoria's life seeped out of her.

"Are those things they said about you—they can't be true," Eleanor said, sounding hopeful the rumors were merely lies.

Victoria wished she could deny it, all of it, but there was no way. She'd shed the moniker of Delilah Goodnight in Defiance. The fancy clothes, the scandalous acts, the upstairs girls, the pink champagne, the life without limits belonged to someone who no longer existed. Folks would never let the reputation die, though, and Victoria knew it.

"It's all true," she said flatly. "If it's any kind of excuse, I thought you'd sold me. Logan saw me one night a few years later but was so drunk he didn't recognize me." And he'd beat her in a drunken rage. That was the night Victoria Patterson had slipped beneath the surface and Delilah had risen in her place. She remembered it well.

Eleanor rubbed her forehead as if a headache was stirring. "Oh, God. This is all my fault. If I hadn't interfered. If I had just left you and Logan alone. You woulda wound up pregnant, but he would have killed anyone who touched you."

Hearing his name out loud squeezed Victoria's heart, and for a moment, she thought she might just curl up in a ball and stay that way till she died. She'd never ever been so devoid of hope, so overwhelmed with gut-wrenching guilt. God, would it ever go away?

And what of their daughter in Stillwater? The girl certainly could never know the truth about her mother.

Victoria flicked a glance at Eleanor—she didn't need to know about Elise. The woman had enough heartache thrust upon her by a wretch of a daughter. News of a granddaughter would only add to it.

"Why are you here now? After all this time."

"Something happened in Defiance." She looked at her hands. She could still recall the feel of Logan's blood on them, hear his last words to her as he lay dying in the street. "Logan found me there. And I loved him every bit as much as I did when I was seventeen. Maybe more. And we were talking about a future." Her voice turned cold with bitterness. "A drunk stabbed him and he bled to death in the dirt and the horse manure." She closed her eyes, unwilling, unable to bear her mother's stunned gaze. "And because of me, twelve men are buried at the bottom of a mine in Defiance. I paid a man to blow it up."

There. It was all out now. No secrets. Her mother knew the harlot and murderer Victoria Patterson had become.

Silence fell. The Regulator clocked on the wall ticked away the minutes. It was a long time before Eleanor spoke. "Do you want to change, Victoria?" she asked softly. "Is that why you're here?"

"Change?" Change meant a future, some kind of way to move forward. That didn't seem possible. But she wasn't Delilah Goodnight anymore, either. "I have changed. The weight of what I've done...those men shouldn't be dead. Logan shouldn't be dead. I should be." There was no holding back the sobs. They raged through her body, shaking her violently, punitively. "I don't know why I came here. There's no place in the world for me." Oh, God, she wondered if she'd ever get through a day without succumbing to this guilt and the grief.

Suddenly her mother's arms were around her and Victoria cried harder. Eleanor held her, stroked her head, rocked her little girl, and whispered soothing words. For just a moment,

Victoria pretended she was eight years old again and nothing terrible had happened in her life. She couldn't hold back the flood of horrible memories for long though.

"I tried to kill myself once," she whispered to her mother. "If I'd succeeded, Logan and all those men would still be alive."

"Oh, no, no, no," Eleanor said, sounding shocked, compassionate. "Don't talk like that." She rocked Victoria and hugged her. "You need to understand something." She waited for Victoria to look up. "Your tears, your guilt, won't bring Logan or those men back. And I'm not gonna let you crawl into a grave right behind them. You hear me?"

"What am I going to do, Momma?" Pain choked her voice, her soul.

"Start over. Start living again."

"I can't. All this death—I can't. It's too much."

"Shhhh." Eleanor laid her cheek on Victoria's head. "We're gonna take this one day at a time. You're home. You're safe, and we'll get through this together."

One day turned into ten. As the gray light of dawn began claiming the day, Eleanor peered in quietly at Victoria. Her daughter lay sleeping, tangled in a shift, most of the covers kicked off. Tendrils of long, auburn hair shot out crazily in every direction. It looked as if she'd been wrestling a bear all night.

Or ghosts.

Eleanor sighed but was empty of tears now. Her and Victoria's pasts were riddled with huge, vicious mistakes, and there was no arguing the consequences had been nearly soul-destroying. But they could get through this. They had to.

God help us...

The newspaper clasped behind her back rustled with her tightening grip. She backed away from the door and once again opened the month-old paper. A headline screamed, "Dozens Dead in Defiance Disaster."

The first time she'd read the article, she'd thought only of the men buried in the explosion. She paid scant attention to the references about the event being a criminal act instigated by Delilah Goodnight. *A horrid woman,* she'd thought, *to put someone up to a heinous act like this.* But her sympathy had quickly drifted back to the missing men, most likely entombed beneath tons of rock.

She'd thought little of the infamous madam's involvement. Murder wasn't such a leap from the other things the woman had reportedly practiced.

Only, *the woman* turned out to be Victoria.

Struggling to take all this in, Eleanor stepped over to their little dining table and dropped onto a chair, shoulders sagging. Thanks to an army of notoriously graphic cowboys, the name *Delilah Goodnight* was as well-known as Custer or Hickock in the scandalous circles. Thanks to what had transpired in Defiance, it would be synonymous with Satan for the next century.

It?

Didn't she mean *her?*

Eleanor's gaze drifted back to the bedroom door. She'd only had the best intentions for Victoria by getting her out of Dodge. To a decent job. A brighter future than what Eleanor could offer. The pretty picture Eleanor had kept tucked away in her heart.

The broken, hopeless thing in there bore little resemblance to that picture. But neither was she the godless, decadent, cold-hearted human train wreck known as Delilah.

Eleanor and Victoria had to try to move on, make something good of the years they had left. If a person dwelled on nothing but regrets, giving up on life was inevitable. Eleanor feared Victoria had come home because she *had* given up and was on the verge of succumbing to those regrets.

A hopeful thought sparked to life in Eleanor's heart. Perhaps Victoria had returned to Dodge because she was ready to be *remade* into something better? Maybe *that* was why Eleanor had stayed put all these years—God knew her daughter would need her one day.

And Eleanor would not lose Victoria again. A fierce sense of protection rose up in her. *I won't, Lord. Please tell me I won't have to. I'll do anything to help her, to keep her safe, see her get her life back on track.*

She folded her hands and bowed her head. "So many mistakes, Lord," she whispered. "Oh, if only I hadn't interfered with her and Logan, maybe none of this would have happened in the first place." The guilt pierced her heart once more.

There is therefore now no condemnation for those who are in Christ Jesus.

The scripture eased some of her regret and she smiled, grateful for the Lord's compassion. The words reminded her their mistakes were a part of a bigger plan. She had to believe that, or she would go crazy. "Guide me, Lord. Help me to know how to help her."

Victoria gurgled, a strange, sad sound, and rolled over. She did not wake up.

She slept. She slept quite a lot, and Eleanor had been giving her some time, but maybe what Victoria needed now was a reason to get out of bed.

The idea felt right. Eleanor would ask around about a job— something that would keep her daughter away from people. Or at least men. She couldn't be recognized. She would need to hide for a long time yet to come.

Perhaps they should move. Living over a saloon was the

worst possible place for Victoria. Eventually someone would recognize her.

One step at a time, Eleanor cautioned herself. *Get her a job first. Give her some place to be, something to do with her time while she heals.* Resigned to taking this slow, she went downstairs to make their breakfast.

Two

VICTORIA BLINKED, grimaced, and clawed her way up to a sitting position in the bed. She could tell by the orange tint in the room and the long shadows it was nearly sunset. *Good. Up just in time to go back to bed.*

She caught a whiff of her body odor and couldn't recall when she'd bathed last. Four days? Five? She hadn't put on any cosmetics since leaving Defiance, and wouldn't. That alone should provide her at least some anonymity. She hadn't been outside in two weeks—no, there'd been a buggy ride yesterday with Eleanor at the ungodly hour of six a.m.

Eleanor had dragged Victoria out of bed at dawn so she could get some fresh air and not have to worry about running into anyone. She appreciated the act, if not the time of day. And she wasn't blind to her mother's sacrifices. She'd given up the only bed in their little two-room apartment to sleep on the cot in the other room.

Awareness, however, was not the same thing as appreciation. Appreciation was an emotion Victoria couldn't muster at the moment. She couldn't muster much of anything. Now that she was home, she felt as if she'd hit some emotional tipping point. She sensed the need to tread carefully because her balance was in a delicate state.

The black leather Bible her mother had set beside the bed seemed too somber, too daunting, to pick up just yet. But she would. Eventually. She had promised Logan. She brushed her fingers over the word *Holy*. God is holy. God hates sin. God loves you.

How could He?

Beneath the Bible sat another book and Victoria picked it up. *The Collected Works of Shakespeare*. A bittersweet memory came to her. Summer nights, the air full of cricket song, and a lamp burning as she read late into the night. Such an innocent escape.

She'd been taken with many of the bard's stories, but the *Merchant of Venice* had drawn her in. She'd read the story of the fiery Portia at least a dozen times. A woman who had thrived in a man's world.

Wanting to revisit a simple, pleasant time in her life, she flipped open the book and let her eyes land at random on a passage.

> *His scepter shows the force of temporal power,*
> *The attribute to awe and majesty*
> *Wherein doth sit the dread and fear of kings,*
> *But mercy is above this sceptered sway.*
> *It is enthronèd in the hearts of kings,*
> *It is an attribute to God Himself...*

Even Shakespeare, through Portia, had pondered God's mercy. Somehow the kinship made her feel better about not reading the Bible yet. This quote seemed to say *It's all right. I'll wait for you—*

The tinkle of silverware from the other room said Eleanor had again prepared dinner and brought it up the stairs. Victoria replaced the books, tied her robe, and opened the door to the other room. It served as their kitchen, parlor, dining room, and Eleanor's bedroom. Furnished sparingly with battered hand-me-downs, the apartment above Big Mike's Saloon reeked of failure and despair.

For a fleeting instant, Victoria lamented the loss of her furs, silks, brass beds, roomy suites, and servants. Only for an instant. This was her life now—such as it was. It seemed appropriate for her—justice—but Eleanor deserved more.

"What's for dinner?" she asked, feigning interest.

"Chicken pie." Eleanor finished setting out the humble place settings of tin plates and cups arranged around a steaming pie.

For the first time in weeks, Victoria's stomach grumbled with hunger. "Smells good." She drifted over to the small, wobbly table and sat. Sprigs of gray hair sprouted out of Eleanor's tight bun. Smudges underlined her eyes. She moved wearily.

The return of the prodigal is taxing her.

Still standing, Eleanor picked up a knife, seemed to ponder something, then cut into the pie and put it on the plates. Victoria picked up her fork and took a test bite.

Eleanor didn't wait for a review of the meal. "Victoria, I've been thinking. It's time for you to get a job."

Victoria felt her eyes bulge and the pie turned to sawdust in her mouth. "A job?"

"I've let you sleep too much, given you too much time to yourself to dwell on things. You need a reason to get out of bed. I need the extra money to get us a place that ain't right over the top of some of your old customers."

Victoria's appetite dissipated like smoke. She swallowed the bite of pie but didn't taste it. "I don't plan on lying around here forever. I'm sorry if I've been a burden."

"You're not a burden. And if you're not planning on lying around, what are you planning on?"

A bullet to the brain. The thought pounced on her like a stalking lion. The idea of ending this misery, this choking weight on her heart, held too much appeal. "I'm not sure yet," she said flatly.

Eleanor smacked the back of her chair then sat, staring boldly at Victoria. Victoria watched her mother wrestle her frustration under control. Finally, huffing, the woman said, "I found you something."

Weary, eager to just climb back into bed and end this conversation, Victoria instead politely inquired about the job. "Tell me."

"GW Moore is a rancher and the publisher of the Dodge City Dispatch. He needs someone to, well, be his eyes for him. He's losing his vision."

Victoria didn't understand exactly, but the effort to ask for more information struck her as Herculean.

Eleanor continued, "His daughter helps him write his editorials and she reads to him. Helps him with his correspondence and whatever else. He stays home, mostly. Comes into town once a week to drop off the column and do his errands for his ranch. He's a nice old man and he don't hang around a lot of people."

"Where's the daughter?"

"Went back to Pennsylvania. School or a boy, I'm not sure which."

Young love? Hope it works out better for her. "I don't think I'm interested. I've never been much of a nursemaid."

Eleanor chuckled. "You don't know GW. Eighty years old and he could work circles around us both." She scooped a bite of the pie. "Besides, I took the liberty of accepting the position for ya."

For an instant, Victoria felt a rage rising in her over her mother's audacity. It died nearly as quickly as it sparked. Victoria's fight was gone...unless she counted the battle to get out of bed every day. And even in that one, she sensed the tide turning against her. Maybe one day, she just wouldn't get up at all ever again. "I'm not fit for decent work, Momma." Not an argument, merely an observation. "I don't know what I'm fit for."

"You're starting over. That means you can do anything you put your mind to."

"Oh, stop it, Momma." Victoria buried her face in her hands. "Stop it. Everything is not going to be sunshine and roses. For God's sake, just leave me alone and let me—"

"Die?"

Victoria didn't answer her, but surely death was better than this.

"No," Eleanor whispered. "No."

Three

MR. GW MOORE was what Victoria would have called a pistol. Here in his elegantly appointed drawing room, the man sat ramrod straight—impressive posture for an eighty-year-old man—and ran a gnarled hand through his shock of silver hair. His bright green eyes betrayed a sharp mind—even if he couldn't see past his nose. His bushy, silver mustache wiggled as she and Eleanor sat down on the settee opposite him.

"Eleanor, is your daughter as pretty as she smells?"

Victoria had known a lot of men in her life and was wise to their wiles. This old goat only sought to charm them, not express a lecherous heart. Before her mother could answer, Victoria tossed her braid over her shoulder and leaned forward. "If you can't see me, it doesn't matter, but we'll go with *prettier*." The little surviving ember of humor surprised her.

The old gentleman chuckled and ruffled his black string tie. "You've brought me a firecracker, Eleanor. Can I keep up?"

"I'm honestly not sure, GW." Eleanor winked at her daughter. "It should be fun watching you try."

For the first time in months, Victoria thought about smiling. In the end, she didn't. "How many hours will you be needing me, Mr.—"

"GW. Call me GW. Everybody does."

"All right."

"And I reckon as many hours as you can stand me. I'm not ready to retire from the newspaper or running this ranch. I've got everything from editorials to write, to ledgers to read, to horseflesh and cattle to assay."

"I don't know anything about judging horses or cattle."

The old man grinned. She only knew because his mustache seemed to spread a little. "You will." He reached down beside his chair and produced a cane. "Let's take a walk."

Not shy about his intended use for Victoria, he clutched her arm and verbally directed her around his home—a comfortable, adobe-style house done up in velvet furniture, Indian blankets on the walls, Spanish tile on the floor. The three of them exited out the patio at the rear of the house.

"Now, I'll show you one of my new projects."

The three of them ambled out toward the corral. Ranch hands scurried around the place like ants, leading horses, driving wagons loaded with everything from fence materials to hay, and trotting off into the prairie after scattered herds. The gentle hills around GW's ranch were peppered with moving dark patches of milling cattle and cowboys whistling and swinging ropes to drive them. Off toward the west, closer in than the cattle, a herd of horses, at least a couple hundred head, grazed lazily in the waist-high grass.

A screaming, ornery horse's neigh snatched her attention back to the corral as they approached.

"Oh, I wish I could see her well, Victoria. I hear she's something." Sadness and awe warred in GW's voice as he leaned on the top rail.

A glistening, muscular bay mare with four white socks

stood quivering on the far side of the corral. Sleek and sassy, she whipped her head about nervously and pawed the ground. A cowboy, blond hair flowing from beneath his sweat-stained hat, hands hanging at his sides, slowly approached the animal. Victoria caught the hint of a hitch in his step and wondered if the horse had caused it.

Suddenly, the horse seemed to decide the man was too close. She neighed angrily again, pinned her ears, and bolted to a new spot, positioning herself against the fence but between the cowboy and the newly-arrived spectators.

Victoria wondered who this extremely patient wrangler was. Tall, heavy with muscle, he moved more like a panther than a man as he pivoted calmly toward the animal. He was, she guessed, a few years younger than she, somewhere in his late twenties. Blond, in need of a shave, but easy to look at with his high cheek bones and dimpled chin, Victoria figured he must have a long trail of broken hearts behind him.

The cowboy paused, seemed to reconsider his interaction with the horse, and suddenly turned away from her. His stride heavier, more determined, but betraying a slight limp, he marched over to his audience. "I need to give her a minute."

"Toby, you know Eleanor," GW said, motioning to the ladies. "This is her daughter Victoria."

Sapphire eyes warm with cheer, he raised and dropped his stained white hat in greeting to the ladies. "Miss Eleanor, I'm looking forward to our next meal with you. Miss Victoria..." His gaze lingered. "It's nice to meet you."

"Is that horse as pretty as Toby says?" the old man asked the ladies.

Victoria thought of her previous answer to the similar question about her. "Prettier."

GW frowned at her, bushy eyebrows colliding. "That your answer for everything?"

"No, just when it's the truth. But what about her feet?"

"Oh, pshaw." He waved in annoyance. "You don't believe that old wives' tale?"

"Four white socks, keep him not a day—" Victoria wagged a finger.

"Three white socks," Eleanor chimed in, leaning on the fence, "send him far away. Two white socks, give him to a friend."

"One white sock," Toby finished, grinning, "keep him to his end."

"And I suppose none of you walk under a ladder either." GW jammed his cane through the fence toward the animal. "Her feet are fine. I hear she's really something to see."

"She is stunning, GW," Victoria said, done teasing. "Simply stunning."

"Maybe I'll take one more run at making friends with her," Toby said, pushing off the fence. Calmly, he strode to the center of the corral. Yes, Victoria caught the hitch in his step this second time.

The horse was a beauty, but Victoria would have to be the blind one here to miss the mean streak in her. Ears pinned impossibly flat, the mare lowered her head and spun her backside around to Toby, positioning for a kick.

Just aching to make his limp more pronounced, aren't you, girl?

"Why isn't she broke?" Victoria asked GW, curious why a four- or five-year-old horse hadn't been under saddle yet.

"Ah..." He pointed a finger to heaven. "Therein lies the project part I mentioned. Toby there isn't trying to break her, he's trying to heal her."

"Heal her?" Victoria quickly looked the animal over. She didn't see any obvious wounds. "What happened to her?"

"She's been abused," the old man said quietly. "Folks too

heavy on the crop. Finally wound up with a farmer over in Lawrence. He flat-out beat her trying to break her. All he did, though, was make her mean."

"Mean?"

GW cut his eyes at Victoria. "You a parrot?"

She nearly smiled again.

"She killed the farmer," Toby answered without raising his voice. "Stomped him into a bloody puddle of sausage." His right hand drifted to his thigh as if it pained him. "To top it off, she's treacherous. She'll let you get close to her, then all of a sudden, she explodes like a cannon and tries to run you down."

Raging against the world, huh, girl? Victoria couldn't deny a certain sympathy for the animal. "She doesn't sound mean. She sounds like she's not going to take it anymore."

GW seemed to think about that for a minute. "Reckon that's one way to look at it."

Worry lines dragged Eleanor's face down as she watched the horse prance and snort. "Horses like that are dangerous. She's liable to kill somebody else. Like Toby there."

"Aw, he's pretty fast, in spite of his bad leg." The old man shrugged. "I don't know. I can't convince myself she's a lost cause. Toby there is the best horse wrangler I've ever had. He doesn't think she's a lost cause, either. She just needs to know..."

"She can trust you?" Victoria offered.

"No, it's more than that." Toby walked away from the horse and joined the group at the fence. "A horse that damaged. It's hard to explain. I'll bring her around, though."

Four

ABOUT TO STEP out the front door, coffee cup in his hand, Toby paused at the sound of an approaching wagon. He moved the lace curtain aside and half-smiled at the new set of eyes GW had hired. Victoria was a sight more appealing than the niece. Sally looked like a librarian. Victoria looked like a misplaced socialite. And he got that more from the way she carried herself than the clothes she wore.

In fact, the plain, simple dress she'd worn yesterday, the auburn hair carelessly braided and running down her back, seemed...like a mask. Like they were tools she was using to hide some truth. Stooped shoulders that tended to pull back and straighten before she realized it. A chin that drifted up before she caught it. She wanted to hide, was trying hard, but a woman like Victoria couldn't keep her head down long. That shimmering hair, unusual amber eyes, and olive skin would attract men or trouble eventually. Maybe both. Still, she belonged here. He understood the need to hide and take time to collect your wits.

He just wished he could pin where he'd seen her before.

That might help him understand her even better. It would come to him. He was sure of it.

Victoria pulled up in front and set the brake. An instant later, Toby sauntered out from the house. "Mornin', Miss Victoria. In case you didn't catch it, I'm—"

"Toby." She didn't offer a smile. "GW up?"

His half-smile slid sideways as he set his empty cup on the porch rail. "You don't come from a ranching life, do ya?" She didn't savvy, and his smile broke all the way. "He's been up since four-thirty, ma'am."

"Oh, and here I thought six in the morning was an unholy hour."

"Not an early riser, eh?"

"I prefer my first peek of morning to come around noon."

Toby mentally tripped on the statement. Something...he couldn't pull the memory out of the cobwebs. "Well, then I'd say you're going to have to do a little adjusting." He approached the buggy and laid his hand on the seat. "I've already gone over the ranch reports with him and we took a ride to look over some stock. Now he's ready for his newspaper business." He raised a hand to assist her down. "I'll put the horse up for you."

She set down the reins and acquiesced to his help. "Thank you." When he set her on the ground, she did not look up, but instead smoothed her skirt. He liked that she was a little coy, a little distant. Gave him a chance to wonder over her flawless, olive skin and pretty, pouty lips. Silky auburn hair in a simple pony tail. The hair, the dress, appealing but wrong somehow—

"This buggy is a rental and I can't..."

Toby heard a pause.

"Afford to keep that up," she finished. "Could GW supply me with a mount or a buggy?"

"He has a surrey he's been known to loan out. It's a spare."

"Oh, well, then I'll ask him about it."

"I'm sure it'll be fine," he said, climbing up into the seat. "I'll come into town and fetch you in the morning."

"That's not necessary," she protested a touch too loudly.

Toby scratched the back of his head and readjusted his hat, amused by her desire for independence. Sometimes, though, it just didn't make sense. "You have some other way of getting your buggy turned back in to the livery and driving the spare surrey?"

She sighed softly. "No. Thank you for your offer. I don't want to put you to any trou—"

"It's no trouble. Just needs doing, is all." Done debating, he released the brake and snapped the reins.

Mulling over Toby's easy but firm manner, Victoria let herself in the house. She found GW in the kitchen having a cup of coffee. The pot and another cup sat on the table in front of him.

"Ah, you're punctual. I appreciate that."

She wouldn't tell him that Eleanor had practically used dynamite to get her up. But she was here now, and the coffee smelled good. "May I?" She gestured toward the coffee, then realized he probably couldn't see her hand. "Coffee, that is."

"Help yourself. Freshen mine if you would?" He slid his cup forward a few inches. As Victoria poured their coffee, something Toby had said came back to her. "If your eyes are going, how did you survey the stock this morning?"

"Same way I've been doing everything else lately. Relying on someone else's eyes for the details."

He didn't sound bitter, only accepting. GW's situation, though, gave her pause. She didn't *not* like Toby but found it easy to be suspicious of him. Because she didn't know him. Did GW?

"Something about that bother you?"

His question surprised her. "Just makes you—"

"Vulnerable. Yeah, and I don't like it. I have to be careful whom I trust."

"You don't know me. What makes you think you can trust me?"

"I trust your mother."

Victoria didn't know Eleanor. Fifteen years was a lot of time apart, but *she* certainly knew her daughter by reputation. "She mention to you she hasn't seen me in a long time?"

"I'm fully aware."

The forthright answer surprised her some.

"Further," he went on, "she told me you have been involved in some unsavory, troublesome ventures."

"Then why would you let me—"

"Because she said you wanted a new start. I'm a big believer in second chances. A lawman gave me one years back. Changed my life. Always said I'd pass the mercy on if I could, and I do when I can."

Second chances. Mercy. Victoria deserved none of it.

She hadn't come here to ponder her miserable existence, however. Determined to move on, or at least appear to move on, she picked up the newspaper on the table. "Why don't you let me do some reading for you?"

"And Toby likes you," he said, ignoring her suggestion. "He's got a sense about people and animals. Says he can see them as they could be, not as they are."

Victoria appreciated the vote of confidence, she supposed, but Toby didn't know diddly squat. Any future version of her was likely to be a disappointment to everyone. "How 'bout that reading?" she asked again.

∾

After a morning of reading in his office, GW asked Victoria to transcribe an editorial on the railroad scandal in Washington. Once that was done, he stood and stretched. "All righty, let's get that into the newspaper—"

"We have to go into town?" Victoria flinched at her panicked tone, which stopped the old man mid-stretch. Going to the livery at seven in the morning was one thing. And she'd taken backroads to get out of Dodge, but he was proposing driving right down Main Street.

GW pursed his lips, obviously pondering her tone, then groped for and plucked his bowler off the back of his chair. "Yes, I think we do," he said firmly.

Victoria bit her lip and rose as well, the editorial wrinkling in her sweaty hands. "All right."

"It's just Dodge. Not an execution."

Victoria wasn't sure she agreed, and her lack of an argument seemed to catch his attention.

"If there's something you're running from, Victoria, things'll only get worse until you stop and face what's chasing you."

Oh, so easy for you to say.

She had brought one of Eleanor's dowdy bonnets with her. It would have to do. If she kept her head down, didn't speak to anyone... "Going into Dodge is fine with me."

"Hmmm." He sounded doubtful. "I get the feeling you'd rather have a tooth yanked out of your jaw, but I'll try to make the trip as painless as possible. Is there maybe someone in particular you're trying to avoid?"

Any man walking? Maybe she was being silly. She hadn't been in Dodge since she'd left. She was practically dressed like a saint now in a drab, brown dress. A far cry from what she used to parade around in. French silks. Custom tailored. Low necklines. High hair-dos. Come to think of it, few men ever really looked at her face.

Except for Logan.

A stab of grief pricked her heart, but she shook it off. "I'll be fine in Dodge. Didn't mean to concern you." She'd never worked in Dodge itself, but there were plenty of men here who had traveled through her various places over the years. Still, the odds any of them would recognize her now had to be in her favor. "I'll be fine."

Five

THE SMELL of manure baking in the August sun greeted Victoria like a slap in the face. The stench and the sound of bawling cattle from the stockyards consumed Dodge City. Nose scrunched against the odor, she skillfully steered GW's buggy up the town's bustling main thoroughfare, Front Street. Used to the smell, the citizens scurried about, mindful only of their business. Men on horses trotted to and fro, pedestrians scurried out of their path. A whip snapped sharply somewhere to Victoria's left. In the distance, the Atchison, Topeka, and Santa Fe announced its impending arrival with a haunting scream.

They drove past a dismal pile of buffalo bones, Peter Dial's Dry Goods & Clothing Shop, G.M. Hoover's Cigar and Liquor store, then the Long Branch. Several men hung around outside, mugs of beer or glasses of whiskey in their hands. Rough-looking and stubbly, most of them tipped their hats to Victoria or nodded. Tugging her bonnet lower, she didn't acknowledge them, but couldn't help a bitter smirk either. Dodge City was as mean a town as the West had spawned, yet it also had the ironic reputation for treating ladies like ladies. Wear a bonnet and a dress with a high neckline, and men assumed much about a woman.

It would only take one man, however, to recognize her and shred every slender thread of her anonymity. She wouldn't forget the risk.

"Ah, summer in Dodge." GW took a deep breath as if he was taking a whiff of perfume. "Smells like money."

"Not exactly how I would describe it."

"The town is alive and vibrant. If it was dying, it wouldn't smell so, uh"—he nudged her with an elbow—"fresh."

She wished it would die. Or she would. Either way, her worries would be over. "Always has been a rowdy town," she said, not really interested in conversation.

GW cleared his throat and changed the subject. "Newspaper office is two buildings down from the Long Branch."

"I remember."

A minute later she pulled the buggy up in front of the *Dispatch*, locked the brake, then hurried around to help her passenger. Scowling, he waved her hands away as he climbed down. "I can't see well, but I still know where the ground is."

She scowled at him. "I'm here to make sure you don't get too close a look at it."

Still resisting her, he moved slowly and stiffly, but once both feet were on the ground, he straightened and tossed out his elbow. "Now you may help me," he said as he slid his cane from the buggy's floor.

Victoria didn't know whether to slap the old man or laugh at him. "You ornery old bas—" She finished the word as a whisper, but he caught it anyway.

"At my age, I am allowed."

"Says who?"

"Says me. And Eleanor would wash your mouth out for such language, young lady."

Twisting down a grin—surprised one even tried to surface —she took his arm and helped him to the boardwalk. "Yes, I suppose she would. I guess I should try to clean it up."

He patted her fingers on his elbow. "If you don't want to draw attention to yourself, yes, you should."

She conceded the point as she opened the door to the newspaper. "Good afternoon, GW," a large, middle-aged woman greeted from her desk at the front of the office. "Mr. Cooley just stepped out. He shouldn't be long."

A gangly, redheaded boy of about twenty or so looked up from the printing press. His left arm loaded with a ream of paper, he nodded at them. "GW, sir, good to see you."

"Good afternoon, everyone. This is my new helper until Sally returns. Please meet Victoria Patterson. Victoria, this is Jenny Renault, our office manager." They exchanged polite nods. "And that is our intrepid reporter, Bobby Barnes."

"Miss."

She hesitated to respond. His eyes gleamed with an eagerness Victoria was all too familiar with. "Mr. Barnes," she said as she removed her bonnet, purposely dragging it in front of her face.

GW reached inside his coat and pulled out his editorial. "Jenny, if you'll see that he gets this and remind him of our editorial meeting Thursday."

She rose at the request. "Will do." She plucked it from his hand and set it on the edge of the desk.

Bobby set his paper down on the press and hurried up to Victoria, hand extended. "Are you new in Dodge, Miss Victoria?"

She let him take her hand and nodded politely, forcing herself not to recoil over his clammy grip or be too obvious about averting her gaze. "No, I'm back after an absence of many years."

"Really? Where do you come to us from? Will you be helping Miss Patterson at the saloon?"

For a moment, Victoria was lost. *Miss Patterson?* GW nudged her slightly in the ribs and the name clicked. A curse word slipped before she could stop it. Bobby's and Jenny's eyes widened. Attempting to play it off, she moved quickly past the blunder. "Miss Patterson. My mother. Of course. I never think of her as Miss Patterson."

"Uh, yes," Bobby muttered.

And in that instant, she saw the judgment in his and Jenny's tight expressions. Profanity said much about a person, and they'd made up their minds about her. Who she was. What kind of a person she was. Well, Victoria had a choice expletive for them both but clamped her jaw on it.

"She's my eyes, Bobby. Jenny. You'll be seeing a lot of her," GW said with a little edge in his tone.

Message delivered. The boss had spoken. The pair nodded stiffly.

A question for Bobby occurred to Victoria. "Why did you ask about me about working at the saloon?"

"Your mother came in and talked to Mr. Cooley about a job for you. I didn't mean to eavesdrop, but it's a small office. I just assumed if you were staying there—at the saloon—you'd be helping out some." *And maybe I'll see you there*, his hopeful expression said.

She didn't like the boy's inquisitive ear or judgmental mind. She liked his assumptions even less. Just how free had Eleanor been with her personal details? Annoyed, she smiled at the boy without a hint of warmth. "You won't be seeing me in the saloon."

∾

Back in the wagon, Victoria looked around at the free-for-all called Dodge. It reminded her of those early years in Oklahoma. From rough hovels in the beginning, she'd doggedly scrimped and saved every penny she could. She'd bought her first house twelve years ago. Finally, in the last decade, she'd been able to build three brothels that would have passed for honest-to-God palaces—though what had gone on inside them had been anything but the stuff of fairy tales.

She'd wielded the power of a queen though. Wielded it foolishly, viciously, never once worrying about whether people respected her. She couldn't have cared less what the Sunday Saints thought of her. To her, people had been mere pawns—valueless, dispensable, but obedient. And one had blown up a mine for her without asking a single question.

She felt GW's stare and realized she'd drifted off. Coming back to the moment, she was about to drop her bonnet back in place when a man's voice from the boardwalk hailed her boss. "GW!"

She and GW both followed the voice and saw a man in a visor and black sleeve stockings hurrying toward them, dodging people on the walk as if he was playing some kind of fast-paced child's game. "GW, good to see you." He ran up to the wagon and the two men shook hands. "We still on for Thursday?"

"You bet ya. Oh…" He leaned back to allow a view of Victoria. "This is my new set of eyes. Victoria Patterson, meet our editor, Mr. Tom Cooley."

Tensed, she offered him a thin smile. Paunchy, with thinning gray hair and a bony face, he regarded her at first with only silence. He started to speak, paused ever so slightly, then went ahead. "Miss Patterson."

But Victoria had seen the question in his eyes. The don't-I-know-you-from-somewhere look. Trying not to be obvious, she lowered her face a little. "Mr. Cooley." Then turned away slightly and put on the bonnet.

"Left the editorial with Jenny," GW said, thumping the floorboard with the cane. "Put this issue to bed and start digging into this railroad news. Oh, and start getting the annual fiscal numbers ready for review."

Mr. Cooley slapped the side of the buggy and stepped back. "Will do. Miss Patterson..." Victoria heard the pause. "Nice to meet you."

"Likewise," she said without much enthusiasm. She didn't recognize the man and was pretty sure he hadn't placed her, but she wasn't certain. Therein lay an inkling of concern. She could see him puzzling it out.

Well, it was a big jump from thinking *maybe* you knew someone to realizing you were in the company of an infamous madam. All Victoria could do was hope Cooley didn't make the leap.

As he walked away, GW leaned in and lowered his voice. "Just what did you used to do, Victoria?"

His question jolted her out of her thoughts. She snapped the reins and drove on for several minutes without answering. He waited patiently, but his stubborn stare drilled into her. Finally, on the edge of town, past the buffalo skinners and with the scent of manure fading, where the volume of the street traffic thinned and she didn't have to yell over the rumbling wagons, she took a deep breath. "Anything you could think of. And then some."

The old man's eyebrow arched in surprise. "Don't sugarcoat it, do you?"

What was the point? Her secret wasn't going to keep in this town.

"Well, women leave that lifestyle all the time. Especially when a cowboy—"

"Delilah Goodnight. My name was Delilah Goodnight." She felt, rather than saw, the tension that drew him back and lifted his shoulders up and away from her. If he knew her name, he knew her reputation, and he probably knew about the disaster in Defiance. It had been in papers across the country. "You know about the mining explosion then?" she asked.

GW turned away to study the hills scorched from the summer heat, all hint of spring gone. Here and there, a lone house or small herd of cattle broke the monotony of the treeless plains. "It was my understanding a man did that."

"I told him to blow up the mine. I didn't mean for him to kill anyone but..." If she'd thought about it, would it have stopped her? She truly wasn't sure. She'd been wallowing in hurt and anger at the time. Still, that was no excuse. "God, what kind of person am I?" Self-loathing backed up in her throat like vomit.

"Only you can answer that, Victoria."

"You want someone else for your eyes?" she asked, too ashamed to look at him.

"No. No, I don't believe I do." He did not add an explanation and she decided to take his decision without questions, without probing as to his thoughts on her. Maybe she didn't want to know.

Six

"I'M NOT FIT to do this work. I'm not fit for any kind of decent work." Victoria couldn't eat and laid down her fork. Her mother's creased brow and wet eyes tugged at her heart. "I wish you'd quit looking at me like that, like you're in pain."

"I am. I ache for you. You've got to forgive yourself."

"I can't." The thought was as alien to her as the spirals of stars in the sky. "I'm alive and some good men are dead. Even the bad ones didn't deserve to die buried alive." Her throat clenching, she rose and marched over to the window. Long shadows reached across the dusty street below. "Maybe I should just walk off a cliff or step in front of a wagon. Put me out of my misery."

Eleanor slapped the table, jostling glasses and silverware. "Fine. Then end it."

Her mother's outburst startled Victoria and she spun around.

Eleanor surged to her feet. "If that's what you really want. Sounds like you've been selfish your whole life. Why stop now?"

"I don't—" Victoria couldn't finish. Eleanor covered her face with her hands, her shoulders shaking with silent sobs.

Oh, God, haven't I hurt enough people? She went to Eleanor and wrapped her in a hug.

After a moment, Eleanor hugged her back. "You've got to stop saying things like that. I can't lose you again."

Victoria blinked back her own tears. "Somehow, I've got to make peace with all this, Momma. How? How do I do that?" If only Logan were here. He'd tell her something about God's love and peace. But he wasn't here, and she had to get used to the idea. Or go crazy.

Eleanor was surprised so much hope could still live in her but now it positively bubbled up like beer foam from a keg as she looked around the empty parlor. She gave Muldoon a twenty-dollar gold piece and nodded at the room, imagining furniture, pictures, rugs. She and Victoria could live here in this quiet neighborhood, away from the saloon, and figure out their next steps. "It'll do."

The fat little Irishman smiled at the coin and tucked it away in his checkered suit. "Well, then, that's that."

"And you keep your mouth shut about where I've moved to." She saw the question in his eyes and thought it best to address it rather than leave him wondering...and making up gossip. "Some of them drunks at Big Mike's have been getting out of hand. I don't need my daughter around such as that. She's a nice girl."

"Oh, well, I can understand that, shore. 'Tis a quiet neighborhood, this one, for the most part."

"Quiet as I can afford anyhow. What about the furniture?"

"It'll be here this afternoon."

He squirmed a touch and Eleanor caught it. "Your knickers in a twist?"

"No, no. It's just that..."

"What?"

"Well, some of the furniture is coming from Rud Cooper's place and..."

"Spit it out, you little leprechaun."

Muldoon's face twisted with indignation. "The settee has a blood stain on it," he said almost defiantly. "Earp was his usual heavy-handed self during the arrest."

"How bad is the stain?"

"Eh, just a drop." He raised a finger and added quickly, "But you didn't pay me to cl—"

"Never mind," she said, her gaze drifting around the room again. A home. With her daughter. "It'll come clean. Most stains wash out with a little effort."

Seven

THE ACCIDENT WAS Victoria's fault. She had her bonnet pulled too low and collided with the young woman exiting the mercantile. Apples and canned goods rolled in a dozen different directions.

"Oh, I'm sorry," she said, feeling more inconvenienced than contrite. She wanted to get in and get out of the mercantile. Tempted to keep going, she knew propriety wouldn't allow it.

Victoria and the woman dropped to their knees at the same instant. Their eyes met and recognition sparked immediately. The pale but pretty face and startling green eyes were familiar. To be sure, though, Victoria scanned the other woman's face and spotted the little scar along the jaw. Millicent. Hoping she had forgotten working for Victoria, or at least would let it go, Victoria began gathering groceries up at a harried pace. The woman stayed stock-still.

"Here..." Victoria dropped the canned tomatoes and some apples in the basket sitting between them. "Again, I'm sorry." She did not meet the woman's gaze.

"I know you know me," she whispered.

Victoria stayed silent, unsure of what to say. Things had ended badly with Millicent. To say *You have me mistaken for someone else* seemed ludicrous. Victoria had put that scar on Millicent's chin with the swipe of a broken champagne bottle. In a rage, she'd honestly tried to kill the woman. Victoria doubted her former employee had forgotten the event or the customer over whom they'd tangled. A senator from Texas.

Millicent's eyes crawled every inch of Victoria as both women slowly rose to their feet. The drab dress, the worn bonnet, the simple auburn braid hanging over Victoria's shoulder told Millicent a story. "My, how the mighty have fallen."

Victoria couldn't bring herself to plead with the woman to keep her mouth shut, neither did she want to sound too hostile. She tried, instead, to sound blandly curious. "What are you doing here? You still in the business?"

Millicent narrowed her eyes. "It's none of your business."

Victoria would take that as a yes, but the way Millicent was dressed—a new but simple, flowery, two-piece outfit, only a touch of makeup, blonde hair neatly swept up, and haggard eyes —said Dodge City wasn't making her rich.

A million things crossed Victoria's mind to say. An apology. A verbal attack. Something to set Millicent off balance. A request to keep this meeting between them quiet. She decided not to tip her hand one way or the other. "Well, I'll be seeing you."

Victoria started to go into the store, but Millicent clutched her arm. "I'm willing to let sleeping dogs lie," she said in a harsh whisper. "I don't have to tell anybody you're in town."

"What do you want in return?"

"Nothing. We just pretend we don't know each other."

Victoria couldn't fathom what Millicent was after. Thinking it best to keep things vague and up for interpretation, she pulled her arm free and said simply, "Don't forget your basket."

~

In spite of their concerns over Millicent, Eleanor couldn't help smiling every time she and Victoria bumped into each other in the kitchen. They were preparing a simple meal of ham, cabbage, and green beans. Simple, but GW had always raved about Eleanor's cooking, and tonight, he and Toby were coming over for dinner in the new place. Everything felt fresh and full of hope to Eleanor. For the first time in years.

She reached for the spoon to stir the beans as Victoria reached over to stir the cabbage. Their hands collided, and Eleanor chuckled.

"You should be worried, Momma. Millicent could tell everyone in town about me."

"Why didn't you ask her not to?"

"I don't know." Victoria tapped the spoon on the side of the pot and set it down. "That part about she didn't have to tell anybody I was here. Letting sleeping dogs lie. She was telling me something about herself."

"I think little Miss Millicent might have a secret of her own." Eleanor put down her own spoon and used her apron to check the ham in the oven. "When she first came to Dodge, she was working out of a crib over on Water Street. Most of her customers were buffalo skinners. Then she got a small place at the end of Smidgen's Row. And she ain't taking customers."

"She's got a man," Victoria said instantly.

"That's the rumor, only it seems to be a secret who he is."

"Then he's someone who's got something to lose."

"Which would be why she wouldn't want trouble with you."

"Too much attention on her."

Let sleeping dogs lie.

Though, in Eleanor's experience, eventually, all dogs woke up. With a little less spring in her step, she finished cooking.

Victoria opened the door to GW and Toby, only to be startled by a large bouquet of roses. The old man lowered them enough to show his Cheshire-cat grin. "For the ladies of the house."

"Why, thank you, GW," she said, taking them from him and hooking an arm through the crook of his elbow.

Toby followed, carrying a bottle of port and a loaf of bread. "I brought the practical gifts."

"I see that. Thank you." Victoria led GW into their small dining room. The place settings were mismatched, even the chairs didn't go together, but the house smelled like heaven. A steaming ham sat in the middle of the table. "Our guests have arrived, Momma."

A moment later, Eleanor appeared carrying the bowl of fragrant cabbage. "Evening, gents. Have a seat."

In minutes, they were settled and dropping napkins into their laps. GW blessed the meal and the company and took a bite of ham. After savoring it, he frowned. "You're just doing this to tease me," he said, taking another bite. "I will make the offer again to come be my cook. I'll pay you any amount you want."

"Ain't about the money. I like my own kitchen."

"Then I will build you a cabin, woman, on my ranch. You'll have your cake and eat it too. And so will I."

"I'm not sure I could stand being that close to you all the time."

"Aw, he's not that bad, Eleanor," Toby said, trying the ham.

He moaned in delight. "And for cooking like this, I'll help him build the cabin."

Victoria listened to the friendly banter and watched the smiles playing on all their faces. Millicent might be going about this very minute spreading lascivious gossip about a notorious madam, but for the next little while, Victoria decided to put away any thoughts of the woman.

Toby washed down a bite with a swig of water and looked at her. "I made a little progress with Delilah today. She had a chance to kick me and didn't take it."

Victoria nearly choked on her green beans. "What did you say?"

"The horse. She didn't kick me."

Victoria's breath hitched. "What did you call me?"

"Not you." Toby's brow furrowed in confusion. "The horse. Her name is Delilah."

Was this some sort of cruel joke? Did GW find this funny? Her profession and reputation amusing?

Apparently her disgust with the choice of names showed on her face. GW and Toby pulled back a little from the table. Toby shrugged a defensive shoulder. "We didn't pick the name. She came to us with it."

"Since it fits, I didn't see a need to change it," GW said, throwing a confused glance around the table.

Victoria let out a breath, feeling a little better but impacted somehow by the coincidence. Logan had never believed in them. A mean, treacherous horse named Delilah. No, that couldn't be a coincidence. Was God trying to tell her something?

What? "A deceitful, vicious female."

"Maybe for now," Toby said quickly, "but I'm working with her. She's got a lot of promise. She'll make a fine horse one day."

"Well, I think I'll get dessert," Eleanor interjected, obviously attempting to move them past the awkward moment. "Who's in the mood for peach cobbler?"

The men nodded and affirmed their eagerness to sample more of Eleanor's cooking. Victoria gave her mother a grateful smile.

Eight

CHARLIE, Oscar, and Lawrence clambered noisily into the hotel lobby, saddle bags swinging, spurs jingling, boot heels thudding on the wood floor. Startled, a young girl, petite and fair with wide, brown eyes, whirled from the mailboxes to face them. Clutching an envelope to her bosom, she smiled shyly. "Can I help you, gentlemen?"

Charlie, the tallest one among them and the youngest—just verging on thirty—pulled off his hat and offered her a fetching smile. Swarthy with dark, inviting eyes of his own, he leaned on the counter, drawing close to her. "Yes, ma'am. We'll be needing a couple of rooms for the night."

"Eh," Oscar growled, shoving him aside. "We got to ask some questions first." A short man with a sickly complexion, he leaned toward the girl. "Any chance you've seen Delilah Good-night in town?"

"Deli—?"

Charlie shoved Oscar back and raised a hand like he was telling a bad dog to *stay*. "Yes, ma'am," he said to the girl, sugar dripping from his voice. "You know of any young women who may have just arrived in town? Probably pretty. A little foul-mouthed, most likely."

The girl frowned. "Not staying here." The very idea seemed to offend her.

Lawrence stood back and watched the interaction in silence but regarded Charlie with a slight scowl, his tight, stubbly jaw expressing controlled anger. Charlie shot him a quick stink eye and leaned on the counter again. "What's your name, sweetheart?"

"Megan."

"Well, Megan..." He drew swirls on the counter with his index finger. "My friends and I are pretty tired from the trail, but if you're up to it later, after I get a bath, I'd like to take you out to dinner."

The girl's eyes rounded and she nervously brushed the bangs off her forehead. "Well, I—uh, I couldn't't."

"Sure you could." With a wink, Charlie spun the hotel register around and commenced signing in.

Victoria peeked out GW's library window and contemplated Toby. In the corral with Delilah, he moved slowly, following her, chasing her with his mere presence. She made two nervous runs around the corral, then Toby suddenly wheeled away from her and limped to the fence. The longer he worked, the more pronounced it grew. He laid both his hands on the top rail and just stood there.

"Why does he do that?" she asked GW, who was sitting at his desk using a gigantic magnifying glass to sort through some papers. "Run her around the pen a time or two, then turn and walk away from her. His leg?"

"Security," he said absently, shuffling a page aside. "Sense of peace. It's the equivalent of giving a tamer horse a carrot. He's teaching her he'll walk away and give her time to rest."

Breathing room, she thought.

She watched him run through the procedure again, but this time, he pushed to get a little closer to her. Delilah did one loop around the pen, then turned and dove for Toby. In a flash, she had her teeth latched onto his side and flung him high in the air like a rag doll.

"Toby," Victoria screamed.

Toby met Victoria as he was coming out of the corral. Limping, banging off the dust with his hat, he let himself out and grinned sheepishly at her as she hurried up to him. "She said she's had enough for one day." His side hurt like he'd been picked up with a vice grip. Getting slammed to the ground didn't do his leg any favors either.

"Are you all right?"

Embarrassed, he was also honestly glad to see her concern. "I'll live. My pride, more than anything, is hurt."

"Well, let's get you inside and take a look."

Moments later, she had him sitting at the kitchen table, shirt pulled up. She winced at the wound: a perfect black-and-blue-and-red impression of horse teeth. She dropped his shirt tail and stood up. "She didn't break the skin. I don't know how." She spun, marched over to the sink, and pumped the handle twice, dousing a dishrag in ice-cold water. "Here. Press this on it."

He took the cloth and did as ordered. "It'll be a long trail with her, but she'll give in."

"Is that what it takes?" Victoria pulled a can of menthol from the cabinet. "She just has to be broken?"

"I've learned to hate that word." Toby hissed as Victoria wiped the smelly paste on his side. He suspected she was enjoying this. "Your hands are cold."

"Sorry, but this will help with pain. And why do you hate the word?"

"'Cause I ain't trying to break her spirit. I see the horse she can be, wants to be. This mean, unpredictable animal—that's a reaction to the cruelty inflicted on her. I want to bring out the best in her."

Victoria capped the menthol. "She's fighting you tooth and nail."

"Just takes time." He started tucking his shirt back in place. "I only want good things for her. She'll come to see that."

Victoria clutched the can in her hands and openly studied Toby as he finished with his shirt. He wondered if she thought he was a handsome man, even with the grime-streaked lines around his eyes and dust in his hair. Couldn't tell the blond from the dirt, he suspected.

"You're gentle and patient. Probably more than anyone I've ever met."

He liked hearing her say that. Maybe more than he ought to. "Thank you." He motioned to his side. "I appreciate the care." Their gazes held for a moment and Toby ducked his chin. "Good hands."

Lord, am I getting in over my head here? Lasso me if I am.

Toby's thanks surprised Victoria because she realized just then that she'd been afraid for him. Seeing Delilah sink her teeth into his side and toss him about like a rag doll had released stark fear in her—honest concern for another human. All the battered and bruised prostitutes she'd doctored, she'd had no feelings for them one way or another. Just their lot in life. Hazards of the job.

This was the first warm, compassionate emotion she'd had for someone other than Logan or Eleanor in what felt like forever.

"You all right?"

Victoria blinked. "What?"

"You're looking at me but *through* me."

"Uh, I..." She waved him off and strode to the cabinet to replace the menthol. "I'm just glad she didn't take a chunk out of you."

"You and me both." He grabbed his hat off the table. "Says a lot about her that she didn't."

"How did you hurt your leg," she asked with her back to him. "If you don't mind me asking? Was it a horse?"

"Yep. I got throwed off the first one I ever tried to train. Hard. She nearly killed me." He hissed inwardly as if recalling the pain. "But I got back up and tried again."

"You've got an optimistic streak a mile wide, don't you?" Victoria wasn't sure if she liked that about Toby or just found it annoying.

"Everything all right in there," GW hollered from the library. "You in one piece, Toby? The way Victoria screamed, I thought maybe Delilah had killed you."

Toby cut his eyes at her as she turned around. Laughter lacing his voice, he said, "No, sir. Alive and kicking, and all my fingers and toes are accounted for." He winked at Victoria. "I had a fine nurse. But I'm done with her for the day—I mean Delilah."

Toby's cheeks flushed over the gaffe and Victoria bit down on a smile. She was surprised she *almost* let it break.

"I'm gonna turn her—Delilah—out, then go help Pablo and the others get that hay in."

"Best get to it then," GW said, "Looks like rain."

Looking at Victoria, Toby drummed his fingers on his hat and opened his mouth to speak, but nothing came out.

She knew exactly what was happening behind those baby blues of his. Men weren't hard to read once you knew the language. His gaze, a little hopeful, roved over her face, then he blinked. He was probably wondering what was the matter with him anyhow? *Gather your wits, Toby.*

He managed to mumble, "Uh, thanks again."

She nodded but didn't say anything. Best not to encourage him. He dropped his hat in place. "Well, I'll see you tomorrow."

Nine

OSCAR AND LAWRENCE asked every customer in the saloon about strangers in town. *Female* strangers. And for every person they asked, it seemed the two required a drink. No one had any information, pushing them to drink even more, apparently to drown their frustration. They were pretty sauced by the time Charlie arrived, having just finished dinner with the pretty little hotel clerk Megan.

Hammered and sloppy, Oscar turned from the bar and sloshed his drink on a young cowboy. The stranger reacted angrily and shoved the drunken sot backward. "Hey, fella, watch it."

Oscar tumbled into Lawrence, causing *him* to spill his drink as well. The three men were chest-to-chest, on the verge of throwing punches, when Charlie stepped between the warring parties.

"Friend," he said to the stranger, "I apologize for my companions here." He snatched a towel off the bar and handed it to the man. "Let me buy you a drink—"

"You ain't buyin'—" Oscar's complaint was cut off forthwith by Charlie forcefully shoving him into his brother again.

"Be quiet, Oscar," Charlie said, scowling at him over his shoulder. His comrade grudgingly obeyed with a loud-and-clear glare. Charlie then smiled amicably at the put-upon cowboy. "A fresh drink smooth things over, friend?"

Wiping at the spill on his shirt, the man nodded thoughtfully. "Yeah. I'd prefer not to bloody my knuckles if I don't have to." He whipped a glance at the brothers. "My apologies, boys. I lost my temper kind of quick."

Oscar and Lawrence maintained their expressions of offense and didn't reply. Charlie grunted. "These two tend to bring that out in folks." He ordered a round for himself and the stranger and waved off the brothers. "Why don't you two go sit in the corner and stay out of trouble?"

Lawrence sidled up, chest puffed out like a rooster. "You can't talk to us like—"

Charlie spun like an angry bull swinging his horns. Oscar and Lawrence actually backed up a step. "You want to find your girl?" Charlie's voice resonated with an ominous, dark tone. "You won't do it if you're in the doctor's office or worse. Now go. Sit. Down."

When the two retreated, Charlie rejoined the stranger who had the whiskey paused at his lips. "You're looking for someone?" the man asked.

"A gal. These boys have a grudge with her. She got a friend of theirs or a brother or some such killed up in Defiance."

The stranger threw back the whiskey, set the glass down. "How do you fit in?"

Charlie shrugged. "The wolverine they're after will more than likely cut off some prized parts before they even blink. I kinda thought the fight would be interestin' to watch."

The man narrowed his eyes at Charlie. "This gal that tough?"

"Mean. Just. Plain. Mean. Slice you and kill you just as soon as look at you." He tossed back his own whiskey, whistled, and hissed as it went down. "Dang. That's not the good stuff. By the way, I didn't get your name, friend."

The stranger pushed his empty glass away, straightened, and turned to Charlie. "I didn't give it." He tapped the brim of his hat in fare-thee-well and sauntered out the door.

Four o'clock in the morning. The new house that Eleanor had rented was nicer than the small apartment over the saloon, but the quiet here was deafening. Only one block off Front Street, it was close enough to the saloons that Victoria could hear some music, occasionally laughter, and all the guns firing. At this hour, however, even the troublemakers were asleep. She sighed and rolled over on her stomach. The quiet would drive her to distraction.

Because it laid her sins bare.

In this pristine silence, crickets sang a gentle serenade. Occasionally, an ambitious rooster added a solo note or two. A horse neighed and flapped his lips down at the livery. Pure sounds that couldn't mask the monster loose in her soul. She needed a raucous saloon to drown out the voices calling her a murderer, to distract her from constant recollections of Logan, and help her ignore the guilt that threatened every second to escape in a sob.

Tears filled her eyes as the scene came back to her for the millionth time. Logan, bleeding to death on the street. Victoria weeping on his chest.

Logan had patted her hand, smearing it with blood. "Promise me...," he had rasped, "promise me you'll give God a chance. Get to...know...Him. Let Him be...your friend."

She rolled over on her side and curled up into a tight, miserable ball. "Oh, Logan," she whispered.

Let Him be your friend...

And she needed a friend so badly. Someone who knew her darkest secrets in detail and still, if Logan was to be believed, loved her. Even Eleanor had been affected by Victoria's past—accepting of it but disappointed her daughter could be so debauched. She was ashamed of her, though Eleanor would deny such a claim.

Tears streaming from her eyes, Victoria laced her fingers in prayer...but couldn't make herself ask for forgiveness.

I can't believe You would give it. Why? Why would You? I don't deserve forgiveness. I deserve misery. I deserve to die.

Her despair taking her to new depths, she sat up. Logan's last request. The only thing he'd asked of her. Get to know Him.

"I can't, Logan. I can't. I'm sorry."

Giving up on sleep, Victoria rose and dressed, harnessed the horse and buggy GW had loaned her, and went for a ride in the crisp air, surprised that fall was hinting at its approach. At sunup, she found herself peering into the corral where Toby was working with Delilah.

Victoria put a foot on the bottom rail and rested her arms on the top one. Toby was standing in the center of the corral with his back to her, hands hanging at his side, waiting. The horse was several feet away, staring at him with curious eyes, slightly-pinned ears. She looked a little less defensive today.

Was that progress? "Is she settling in?"

Toby didn't react to Victoria's question, but she knew he

knew she was there. She felt she'd misstepped though, by speaking, and waited quietly.

"I thought you weren't an early riser," he said finally, softly.

She matched his tone. "This morning, I am." Being here was better than wallowing in her misery in bed. And if she was here, maybe she wouldn't think about trying to cut her wrists again. If Logan hadn't stopped her that time, would he still be alive?

Toby took a small step toward Delilah. The horse defiantly bolted to the far corner.

Maybe not much progress after all.

Delilah swung around and faced Toby, pawing at the ground, head lowered, warning him to stay away. *If she could only understand,* Victoria thought. *He means her no harm.*

Rubbing his thigh, Toby gave up on the horse for the moment and strolled over to the fence. Delilah took a step after him, as if considering a sneak attack, but didn't follow through. Victoria had no doubt he was aware the horse had moved, but he didn't let on and kept his stride steady.

"Fall is coming quick," he said, flexing cold fingers. "By the way, I met some fellas at the saloon last night. They said they were looking for someone."

"And?" She stared past him, watching Delilah twitching her ears...in confusion? The horse almost looked as if she was wondering why he had walked away.

"I don't know. I just had a feeling they might be after you."

She snapped back to him. "What would make you say that?"

"According to one of them, this gal got a brother of theirs killed. They're looking to even the score."

"And that made you think of me why?"

"You're hiding something or running from something. I saw that right off." Sucking air through his teeth, he turned around and leaned back on the fence, shoving his hands into his pockets. "I don't know, to be honest. It's a leap. And I wasn't sure I was even gonna mention them. But the way you reacted to Delilah's name..." He nodded his head like a man forming a firm conclusion. "You're her."

Victoria dropped her forehead on her hands. If Toby could figure it out, it wouldn't take the whole town of Dodge long.

"You know, I met you once," he began. "Lord, must be ten years or more. I was still wet behind the ears, and some of the cowboys I was working with decided they needed to introduce me to...uh, the finer things in life."

"So they brought you to see me," she said, painfully familiar with this story.

He laughed and hung a boot heel back on the rail. "You were working at a place in Oklahoma then. These boys pooled their money and paid for you specifically to entertain me. I took one look at you, all wrapped up in this thin, filmy, silky material —" He cut the air with a long, high whistle. "I ran like a scalded dog. Didn't quit running till I was back in Texas. You scared me straight back to my family."

"How old were you?"

"Oh, sixteen, I guess."

"And was I that appalling?"

"Oh, no, ma'am." He hung his head and chuckled like a man with a secret. "You looked like one of them Greek Goddesses. Way too much woman for a boy. I wasn't ready."

"And yet you remember me?" She was astonished at his memory.

"The first time I met you, you didn't have on any lipstick or eye mess. I think you hadn't been out of bed long." Implying that her disguise had actually betrayed her. Toby worried his lip for a moment, then eased his way back out into the center of the corral. "I saw you in Denver a few years after that. You were wearing, I reckon, everything a woman can put on her face. I wouldn't have knowed you except the boys tried again to get their hundred dollars back from you."

"I didn't pay, did I?" Of course she didn't.

"No, ma'am. You said no refunds." He smiled over his shoulder at her. "You bought us a round of drinks, though." He returned his attention to Delilah, who hadn't moved. "You don't put anything on your face, maybe that will be enough to keep your secret. For a while. You're prettier without it anyway." He took one slow step toward the horse.

Victoria appreciated the compliment but was more interested in the observation. True, most people had only seen her dressed to kill. Everything from kohl eyeliner to red lipstick to provocative silk dresses with low necklines and big bustles. In fact, her necklines had been so shamefully low few men ever even looked at her face.

Except for Logan.

Still, even he hadn't recognized her in Defiance—what, with all the makeup and the passing of the years. "Did these men say where they were from?"

"Didn't ask."

"What do you want to keep quiet?"

Toby's shoulders tensed. His hands curled into fists. He retreated a few steps from the horse, as if he didn't want her to catch wind of his attitude. "You think I want to blackmail you?" he asked without turning.

"Why else would you try to identify me and tell me about those men?"

"Maybe"—he rounded on her then—"I just wanted to do the decent thing so you'll watch your back."

His eyes blazed and Victoria realized she'd insulted him. She never could read the good ones. "I'm sorry. I will keep an eye out."

He dipped his chin curtly and swung back to Delilah, a little too abruptly, and the horse pranced nervously.

"I'm not going to mention this to Eleanor, Toby. She's got enough—" *To worry about with Millicent?* "On her plate, what with the new house and all."

"All right, if you think that's best."

Ten

ELEANOR WIPED the last glass clean and set it on the counter. Big Mike's was empty at the moment. Four in the afternoon. 'Bout the slowest the saloon got. It would pick back up at six, but she was getting off in another hour.

Big Mike's wasn't known for pretty, young barkeeps, upstairs girls, or high-stakes poker games. The new owner had changed it into a quiet place now where reasonable men could get a quick bite from the kitchen or have a few beers then head on home. As such, it wasn't the hub of gossip in Dodge City anymore, but that didn't mean there wasn't any at all. Millicent, however, was keeping details of her love life pretty well-guarded.

When Jacinta came in at five, Eleanor untied her apron and handed it over to the plump Mexican gal. "You get a chance to ask your friend my question?"

"*Sí*," she said, tying the cover at her waist. "She has seen Millicent's friend only once. He is an Americano with a funny, round hat."

"That's it? That's all she could tell you?" Over a week of waiting for this information and this was it?

"I asked her to keep watch. Let us know if she got a better look, but the man only comes at night."

Eleanor rubbed her neck. Victoria was right. Whoever the man was, he didn't want to be seen with a soiled dove. Now who in Dodge would care about that?

Eleanor smiled grimly. She didn't know, but she was going to find out if it took a month of Sundays.

Charlie and Megan exited the hotel and strolled down the boardwalk, a cool evening breeze ruffling her fair hair. "My pa doesn't care for you. Says you ride with a rough crew?"

"What?" His hand flew to his chest. "I'm wounded. Your pa judging me by the company I keep. That ain't very Christian."

"Those two—Oscar and Lawrence—they don't seem very nice."

"Ah, they're a little rough around the edges, but they're good boys."

"He says all you do is hang around in town and cause trouble."

"They hang around. I actually win a little money at poker."

"I'm not sure I'd tell Pa that. He says you got no ambition."

"I have plenty of ambition."

"Pa says you're just toying with me. That I don't mean anything to you."

"Your pa does a lot of talking," Charlie said irritably. "So far, none of it suits me."

"Well, I don't listen to most of what he says. He tells me I'm a handful all the time." Blushing like a new bride, Megan laced her fingers in front of her and shrugged her shoulders shyly. "Nice night for a walk."

Charlie brightened instantly. "Yes, ma'am, it is. I could use a little dinner first. Let me treat you. Again. Dinner with you is becoming a habit. One I don't mind."

She nodded and glanced up at Charlie through long, dark lashes. "I could eat."

They meandered along for another moment when Charlie asked, "You still ain't heard anything about new girls in town?"

Megan snapped her fingers. "Gee, I almost forgot. The lady who does the hotel laundry works part-time at Big Mike's Saloon. She happened to mention Eleanor's daughter. When I asked about her, Jacinta said she's only been here a few months."

Charlie frowned. "Who's Eleanor?"

"The head barkeep at Big Mike's. And you said your friends were looking for any young ladies that might be new in town. I mean, I know she's been here a while—"

"Daughter, huh? A few months?" Charlie scratched his chin. "Timing would be about right. Funny, we—I mean, *they* —they were fixing to ride out. Oscar and Lawrence. Be funny if it was her, after all the time we've spent here looking. I'll be sure to tell them."

"You weren't planning on leaving so soon were you?" she asked, again wielding the eyelashes.

Charlie chuckled. "Not a chance, honey, not a chance." He gave her a huge smile, showing a row of fine, white teeth. "Especially now that I've got something to stay for."

Megan blushed again, the color blossoming in her cheeks.

~

Oscar and Lawrence had apparently lost their patience. No one at Big Mike's Saloon knew a Delilah and the little chubby Mexican girl behind the bar assured them Eleanor's daughter was a nice girl. Getting no leads and nearly broke now, they decided to drink up a storm and unleash it with a fury.

Three bottles in, they commenced to busting up Big Mike's. Most of the patrons of the establishment launched for the door. The poker games ended abruptly. The bartender ran for the law.

"Dang it, I know she's here," Oscar yelled and tossed a chair into the shelves of liquor behind the bar. He smiled drunkenly over the satisfying cacophony of crashing, shattering glass.

Lawrence grimly picked up his own chair and threw it through the front window. Glass exploded out onto the boardwalk. The exertion, however, threw him off balance for a moment, and he swayed in the wind like a tree on a breezy day. Grunting, he staggered over to a chair and sat down hard. "We'll find her."

"Not if you're in jail."

Wide-eyed and wobbly as baby owls, both men looked up at the door. Charlie stood there, his expression dark as a thundercloud, his arms resting on the batwings. Scowling, he peered around the saloon. "If she comes into town, she's gonna hear you're looking for her, especially with this kind of situation. So you're fortunate our little hotel clerk might have found her for us." His gaze shifted sharply to the left and he lowered his voice. "Earp's on his way."

Oscar and Lawrence surged clumsily to their feet.

"Word is he'd rather see trash like you in jail than cut any slack, so you let me do the talking," he said firmly. He stepped away from the doors and waited for the lawman with his hands up. "Marshal."

A moment later, a man in a black, flat-brimmed hat peered over the tops of the doors. His penetrating blue eyes made Oscar and Lawrence shift uncomfortably as he surveyed them and the damage in the room. "Boys, you're in a heap of trouble." He spoke over his shoulder to Charlie. "You know these two?"

"Yes, sir, and I apologize for them." He stepped up beside Earp. "They don't have the sense God gave a goose, and I should have kept an eye on them, but I was enjoying the company of that pretty little clerk from the hotel."

Earp raised an eyebrow at Charlie, expressing obvious disinterest.

"I'm just saying," Charlie hurried on, "if you're agreeable, I can see to it they pay for the damages and ride out." He shrugged sheepishly. "I'd kinda like to stay around a few days and these blockheads are making it too hard."

Earp leaned back and looked down the boardwalk. "Big Mike, how you feel about that?"

The bartender, an old, jittery, gray-haired fella, poked his head around the corner of the building. Twice. Like a wary chicken. Then he slipped out of his hiding place and stepped up beside Earp. Earp opened the batwings for him and the bartender hesitantly walked inside. His stare bounced all over the saloon, but in only a few seconds he was back outside with the marshal. "It's a good hundred, hundred-and-fifty dollars' worth of damage."

"What'll it be, boys?" Earp asked Lawrence and Oscar.

Both men looked straight at Charlie. He nodded. "I'll see they pay, Marshal. And I'll get 'em out of town myself."

Earp grunted. "Friends like that, you don't need any enemies." Before Charlie could reply, Earp was striding away. "Let me know, Big Mike, if they give you any more grief."

"They won't, Marshal," Charlie hollered after him. "I'll make 'em do right."

~

Eleanor figured she was just about willing to do anything to protect Victoria. She had her daughter back. She would keep her safe, her identity a secret. And one way she was going to do that was to find out who Millicent was playing tickle with for the leverage.

She hugged her wool cape tighter and peered out from behind the scrubby pine. A huge harvest moon washed Millicent's simple, one-room cabin in silvery light. The amber glow of candles or a fire flickered invitingly behind one curtain.

Lord, it's cold out here. And I'm getting tired of this. I don't want to still be standing behind this pine tree when the snow starts flying next month. Please let our mystery man finally show up tonight and save us all a bunch of misery.

Perhaps she shouldn't speak to the Lord so, but she hoped He might appreciate her sense of humor.

Apparently, He did. A moment later, a horse and rider approached Millicent's. The man, his face hidden in the shadows beneath his bowler, scanned the quiet street, dismounted, and led his horse around back. Eleanor almost slapped her hands together with victory.

She waited another few minutes, until she saw the light in the window flicker with movement and knew the man was inside. The houses around Millicent's were all dark and quiet. Yes, these respectable neighbors were in bed because the hour was late and they wouldn't see her. Slipping out from her hiding place, Eleanor quietly hurried across the street and up to the front door.

She listened for a moment to the hushed voices on the other side. Millicent's tone was light, clear, and happy. The man sounded more measured, more somber. Eleanor couldn't hear well enough to determine if she might know his identity.

But she would know it tonight.

She raised her hand and pounded on the door, then pushed

into the simple living room bathed in firelight. Millicent sat on her brass bed, her robe pulled closed.

At the fireplace, Tom Cooley stood warming his hands. He jerked up ramrod straight at the intrusion. Surprise, recognition, then fear tensed his expression. "What are you doing here?"

Eleanor grinned, flush with victory. "I need to speak with Millicent."

"I wasn't here." He wagged a finger at her. "You didn't see me. Understand?"

Eleanor shrugged noncommittally and waited for Millicent to say yay or nay. After a moment of chewing on her lip, the woman grabbed Eleanor's arm. "I'll be right back, Tom. This doesn't concern you."

The two women stepped outside in the cold and moved a few paces away from the front door. "He doesn't want anybody to know about me, Eleanor. He said it wouldn't look right for a newspaper editor to have a...a kept woman."

"You don't say anything about Victoria, and I won't say anything about who you're setting up house with." Eleanor leaned in a little and lowered her voice. "I don't care who you spend time with. I just don't want you making any trouble for my daughter. Make trouble for her and it will rain on you too. You can see that, can't you?"

Millicent glanced quickly at her door then back to Eleanor. "Fine. I don't want any trouble. Tom treats me nice and pays my bills and I don't have to take customers."

"Then Victoria doesn't look familiar to you, does she?" It was no question.

"She doesn't remind me of anyone. Especially not the madam who gave me this scar"—she tilted her chin, trying to present her face to the moonlight—"trying to cut my throat."

Eleanor shifted uncomfortably, ashamed of her daughter.

Lord willing, that side of Victoria was gone. "I guess you don't have to worry about it. Delilah's dead."

Millicent's eyes widened a touch, but she pursed her lips and nodded. "Good enough."

Victoria stood by the fire in GW's library and waited for him to finish going over the newspaper's books with his painfully large magnifying glass. She'd offered to help, to either read aloud to him or use her own sordid bookkeeping skills to assess the books, but he'd turned her down.

She saw him weakening, however. Blinking, squeezing his eyes shut. The fatigue was getting to him.

Finally, he laid down his glass and pushed back from his desk. Rubbing his eyes, he leaned his head back on the plush leather chair. "All right. I'm done. It's too hard on my eyes. You said you know some accounting. There you go."

Within a few minutes, she found several questionable entries. By early afternoon, she was sure Tom Cooley was stealing from his employer and wasn't very clever about hiding it.

Eleven

THE WEEKLY MEETING at the newspaper between GW and Cooley came around once again. Normally boring, Victoria couldn't help but think this one was going to be a touch more interesting. The old man had told her he was going to have harsh words with the editor. Not only was he playing fast and loose with the paper's books, Cooley'd had the audacity to disagree with his employer publicly. He'd written several opinion pieces that were diametrically opposed to GW's positions on important local and state matters.

Cooley looked up from a notepad he was writing on as GW and Victoria entered. "Time for our meeting already?" He glanced over at the clock on the wall. "Don't know where the day went."

GW leaned his cane on the desk and dropped into the chair directly opposite the editor. Victoria lingered in the background, since she was supposed to be merely eyes for GW, not some kind of audience or jury.

"Let's get to the meat of things, Cooley," GW said, pulling a cigar from his pocket. "You and I have problems."

"When you hired me, GW, you said I had leeway to editorialize. I could have my own opinions."

GW lit the smoke and set the extinguished match on Cooley's desk. Frowning slightly, the man promptly plucked it up and set it in a coffee mug.

"Did you think you could hide the numbers forever? Or did you think I just wouldn't look?"

"I don't know what you're talking about."

GW puffed on his smoke and exhaled slowly, taking his time. Cooley tried to act calm, but Victoria saw the slight twitch in his brow.

"You can either explain why the books for this newspaper are five thousand dollars out of balance, or you're fired."

"F-five thousand dollars?" Cooley stammered. "Fired? For what? I haven't stolen your money."

"Either you can't do basic math, or you're a thief. Victoria found your errors almost immediately."

Cooley's face tightened like a boiler under pressure. "And just what kind of bookkeeping experience do you have, Miss Patterson?"

She took a moment to try to read his mind—or at least his beady, dark eyes. What did he know about her? "I used to run my own business. A very successful one."

The light of recognition flickered across his face and she got a sinking feeling in her gut. GW took one last puff and then crushed his cigar out in the mug on Cooley's desk. "Here's what we're gonna do, Cooley. I don't like scandals. You've got one chance to make these books right—put back the five thousand dollars that I'm missing."

Cooley ran a hand through thinning hair. His scalp glistened with sweat. "I didn't steal anything. You're taking the word of a two-bit harlot over mine?"

The air in the room seemed to pick up a charge, as if a storm was forming on the prairie. Like a rising thunderhead, GW slowly stood. "Apologize to the lady."

"Lady?" Cooley practically yelped. "You can't tell me you don't know who she is." He surged to his feet and pointed an accusing finger at Victoria. "She's Delilah Goodnight. A harlot. A Jezebel. A godless, immoral—"

GW tossed out a beefy fist and clocked Cooley right in the middle of his mouth. Blood flowing over his lips, the man screeched like an injured cat and stumbled back from his desk, knocking over his chair.

GW shook his hand as if the punch had hurt him more than his target. "You're doing like you do in those editorials—shooting your mouth off without thinking. You're fired, and I'll be pressing charges for embezzlement."

The man scrambled to pull a handkerchief out of his pocket. He snatched it free and pressed it to his lips, all while sharing a baleful glare with GW and Victoria.

Victoria rushed to GW's side and clutched his arm. "GW..." She implored him with her eyes to think about the gossip this would cause. "The scandal wouldn't be good for either of you."

Or her.

His grizzled old face softened, and he tapped her fingers gently. He turned his attention back to Cooley and spoke with more reserve. "Square the books away. Bring the money back, and maybe you'll keep your job."

"I haven't stolen anything."

"Then you are a poor business manager and you should be fired for that alone. I can replace you and have Victoria come do the books." GW snatched up his cane from the desk. "You've got one chance to make things right."

Cooley didn't utter another sound, and Victoria thought she and GW should leave the man to think things over. "Come on, GW." She took his arm and he grudgingly allowed her to steer him from the newspaper office.

Sick that hard feelings had escalated to violence because of her involvement, she ushered GW on outside and to the passenger side of their buggy.

"Don't look so downcast," GW told her as she settled in beside him. "He had that coming."

Victoria snapped the reins. "It was worse than it had to be, because of me. He loathes me, yet I'd be willing to bet he paid some of my establishments' regular calls."

"I expect he did, the low-down hypocrite. And I expect I'll wind up firing him in the end, but I want to see if he'll put the money back."

In spite of this mess and where it would most likely lead, Victoria had to admit she was impressed with GW's vigor. "If you can't see, how did you aim that punch so well?"

He flexed his fingers, bruised and a little scraped. "There was a time I would have planted my fist exactly where I wanted it to go. Truth be told, I was a touch low. I was aiming for his nose."

"I should thank you regardless. It was chivalrous of you to defend my long-gone honor."

He tugged at his tie. "Well..." He cleared his throat and changed the direction of the conversation. "Never hit a man in the mouth if you can help it. Teeth are rough on your knuckles and can cause infection."

Victoria reached over and patted his knee. "I'll clean you up when we get back to the ranch."

Again, the emotions roiling in her heart surprised and puzzled her. Gratitude. Concern. A willingness to be a nurse-maid to an old man.

She snuck a peek at him, curious about this mysterious old man who threw one heck of a punch. Misreading her expression, he winked jovially at her. "He'll keep his mouth shut. Don't worry about Cooley."

Unfortunately, if Victoria knew anything, she knew a man with wounded pride was as dangerous as a wounded bear.

~

"You shouldn't play cards angry, friend." Grinning coldly, Charlie dragged the pile of coins and bills over in front of him.

Cooley slapped his worthless poker hand down on the table. "How do you know I'm angry?".

"Lucky guess," Charlie answered with obvious sarcasm.

Huffing loudly, Cooley flopped back in his seat. "I *am* angry. I fear I am about to be bested by a prostitute."

"Now that *would* be downright embarrassing."

"I knew I recognized her the first time I saw her with GW," Cooley said, gingerly touching his puffy lips. "But my gal told me for sure. Had to beat it out of her, but she told me."

Charlie was reaching for the cards but froze. "Am I supposed to know who you're talking about?" When Cooley didn't answer right away, he finished the task of gathering his winnings and started shuffling the deck.

"Delilah Goodnight."

Charlie's hands faltered for an instant and some of the cards spilled from the shuffle. He cleared his throat and started over, the flutter of the deck rhythmic and slick now. "Why do I know that name?"

"You probably know *her*. She's been a madam for over a decade—a very successful one, and she's run some downright decadent places."

"Didn't she have something to do with a mine or...?"

"Some fella that worked for her blew up a mine in Defiance. Twelve men died."

"Yeah, her." Charlie released a disgusted-sounding huff. "I know some people who want her head on a platter for that."

"Well, send 'em my way. I'll be happy to tell them where she's hiding."

Charlie languidly dealt cards back and forth between them. "I'm listening. And I'm real interested."

Twelve

FROM THE MOMENT of her arrival, going anywhere in Dodge had spooked Victoria. The weekly trips in with GW hadn't made things any better. So many folks waved and greeted him. He was a man who garnered much attention.

As she drove them down Front Street, she surreptitiously studied the faces passing by, especially of the men. Had Cooley spread any gossip? He'd been warned about the books at the paper nearly a week ago, plenty of time to stew over the hurt ego and spread the news.

On the street, however, no one paid her any attention. She didn't see evidence anything had changed.

Tired of these worries nipping at her skirt, Victoria squared her shoulders and lifted her chin. She wouldn't live in fear. If her secret came out, she'd deal with it. For Eleanor's sake, she hoped it didn't.

As if to pile on doubts, Millicent stepped out of the mercantile. She and Victoria looked at each other for an instant, but the woman quickly averted her bruised eyes and strode on down the boardwalk.

He'd beat her. Over Victoria? She should have known there was no way this secret was going to keep. Between Millicent and Cooley, it was as good as printed in the paper.

"You should try smiling, Victoria," GW said in a playful tone. "You got a pretty face. Smiling would only improve it."

"I wouldn't want to draw attention to myself by being too pretty."

His smile faltered, and she regretted her hard tone.

Toby had followed them into town to see the barber and the three had agreed to meet for dinner at the Dodge House. As Victoria pulled up in front of the newspaper office, the ranch hand rode on by.

She did not wave, but GW flipped up a hand. "Get a shave while you're at it, son. You're looking scroungy."

"Will do, sir."

Victoria watched Toby ride off as she absently assisted GW down from the wagon. Willing to keep her secret, not lord it over her. She couldn't figure him. A puzzle she couldn't solve today, she willed her attention back to GW. He, too, apparently had no interest in punishing her for her past mistakes. He'd even defended her honor to Cooley. Chivalry worthy only of Don Quixote, but endearing nonetheless.

Their benevolence these past few months still mystified her. In the beginning, she'd expected them both to either weary of her at any moment or, worse, expect something from her based on her past vocation. Yet they'd been nothing but gentlemen.

Distracted by her ponderings, she did not notice the two men sitting on the bench in front of the newspaper until she and GW stepped up on the walk. Instantly, she knew they were waiting for her and her grip involuntarily tightened on his arm.

The pair, reeking of alcohol, rose slowly. One—fat, balding, and sporting a sickly yellowish complexion—spoke first. "You're Delilah, ain't you?"

GW straightened to his full, still impressive height and stamped his cane. "Gentleman, I believe you must have my assistant confused with someone else."

The second man surveyed Victoria top to bottom and back again. He was quiet, more deliberate than the other man and, she sensed, more dangerous. "No," he said ignoring GW, "you're cleaned up, no paint on your face, but it's you. And we've come for justice."

GW flicked his wrist in a movement so fast Victoria was astonished at the old coot's speed. Before she could blink, he was pressing a derringer to the man's forehead. "I said you're mistaken. Now back off." The stranger's eyes widened slightly, but he didn't move. Beside him, his comrade moved to reach for his sidearm. GW cocked the over-under derringer. "I'm losing my sight, but I ain't blind yet. Your friend there twitches so much as a pinky I'm gonna drop *you* first, then him."

The man waved a hand. "Don't touch it, Oscar." Oscar hesitantly lowered his hand.

GW waggled the gun. "Get out of here. I see either one of you again—"

"What have these two done now?" Another man hurried down the boardwalk, tall and skinny, dark, greasy hair hanging from beneath his hat. "My apologies."

GW glanced quickly at the approaching stranger but did not move his revolver. His hand, steady as an oak branch, had its target picked out and wasn't changing midstream. Victoria realized with a jolt her employer had his own past.

"These boys friends of yours?"

"Not if I shouldn't admit to it."

"You shouldn't."

Seemingly concerned GW might do something foolish, the stranger rushed to interject himself between him and the two troublemakers. "I'm Charlie Smith. Oscar and Lawrence here got a little tight at the saloon several days back. Broke a few things. We just paid the owner in full and now these boys are movin' on."

"You're not going with them?"

"I ain't been in no trouble."

"You keep hanging with the likes of these, you will be." GW seemed to mull over the situation for a moment then grudgingly lowered his weapon. "I see you two again, there's gonna be hell to pay."

The two men behind the greasy stranger glared at GW. Their friend rounded on them and ushered them down the walk like annoying children. "Come on, boys, that's it. You've worn out your welcome in Dodge. Time to head back to Defiance."

Defiance?

Victoria's heart lurched madly at the mention of the town, but she tried not to show her alarm. Beside her, GW hung his cane on his forearm and tucked the spring-loaded derringer back up into his sleeve. A common gambler's weapon of defense. He didn't strike her as any gambler, though.

What he was, was an innocent bystander. Yet another victim caught in her wake of destruction. "I'm sorry about that, GW. Trouble seems to follow me." Or was she, in truth, the creator of it?

He shrugged his shoulder, tugging on and adjusting the sleeve gun. "They said Defiance."

Yes, they said Defiance.

Because a hired man had actually committed the crime, the sheriff in Defiance had opted not to pursue charges against Victoria. His reason, he said, was to give the town a chance to heal. Now, nearly three months later, with the story splashed across front pages from one side of the country to another and vengeful citizens hunting her down, Victoria wondered if Marshal Beckwith was regretting his decision. How were things in Defiance? Had there been any healing?

If she was being hunted by men like this, she'd guess no.

So, there could be more coming for her. "Toby warned me about them. I didn't think they'd find me."

"Only a few people know who you are," GW muttered, "and where you're working. I haven't talked. Your mother wouldn't talk. I can't think of—wait, you said Toby warned you?"

She refrained from hanging her head in shame—barely. "He recognized me."

GW rubbed his chin but quickly dismissed the idea. "Nah. He wouldn't talk. But somebody did?"

"Are you sure about Toby?"

"Positive."

Victoria knew it was a foolish question. There were only two people in town who might have run their mouths. "I'd say it was Cooley."

"Cooley."

"Had to be." Somehow, she knew Millicent, when it came down to it, wouldn't be the one to spread this news all over Dodge. No, this reeked of Cooley.

GW's gaze slid to the front of the newspaper office. "He worked for me for five years, but there was always something..." He trailed off and shook his head. "Not quite genuine. And he did react like a keg of dynamite to your involvement. I thought it was because of your accounting background."

"Maybe it was. Maybe it wasn't. Bet I could find out which and what he's done with your money," she offered hesitantly, knowing how easy it would be to manipulate the man.

"No. I wouldn't want you to do anything...anything..."

"Sordid? It's not like a few flirtatious remarks would sully my reputation, GW," she said bitterly.

"Victoria..." He turned to face her, his expression kind, gentle. "If you want to leave that life behind, start over, then don't start by crossing any lines."

She appreciated his respect and his advice. Both humbled her.

"Besides," he added, "I think I know what he might be stealing for. Local gossip is gambling debts." He patted her on the shoulder. "I've given him a chance to put the money back. Keep it quiet. We'll see what happens. Now, let's go have a steak."

At dinner, GW mentioned the rumor of gambling debts to Toby. "Any truth to them?"

"I've heard the same stories." Toby cut a clean slice of steak. "Enough liquor in him, Cooley talks a blue streak. I can get him to talk about money—his and yours."

"You get him to 'fess up. I'll give him another few days to make things right and then press charges if I have to." GW took a sip of coffee and mulled things over for a minute. "Victoria, if he told those two fellas, then your cat is out of its bag."

The news laid a tense pause over the table. "Who else has Cooley run his mouth to?" she wondered aloud.

GW bounced his fork in his hand and tried to move past their concerns. "I guess we'll know soon enough. I have to fire him, Victoria."

"I know you do."

"Much as it's up to me, I'll keep it quiet."

In other words, Cooley was under no such obligation.

"Bobby Barnes will act as editor until I find someone—unless Barnes proves to have wisdom beyond his years. He's young, but he might surprise me." The old man wiped his mouth then dropped his napkin on his plate. "Well, if you two will excuse me, I need the table to have a quick powwow with the marshal here in a minute. Toby, why don't you take Victoria for an evening walk? Meet me at the buggy in about half an hour."

The suggestion sent a jolt of fear to her heart, but she was also tired of worrying about being recognized. Part of her wanted to go stand in the middle of the street and announce her presence with a shout. She'd been run out of towns before. She could take it.

But not Eleanor. Eleanor had been through enough.

As she and Toby stepped outside, the idea of putting herself out of this misery whispered to her like a siren song.

The day in Defiance when she'd tried to kill herself beckoned to her. Right after hearing about the mine explosion. The weight of all those deaths had crushed her, driven her to her knees in defeat, and then to a straight razor across her wrists.

The memory played vividly in her head for the millionth time, like a player piano stuck on a magical, hypnotic tune.

Logan showed up out of the blue and found her with the razor and the fresh blood glistening on her skin. *"Delilah, please, if someone has to die to give you peace..."* He picked up the razor, the stained blade glinting in the summer twilight. *"Let it be me."* He set her injured arm in her lap, put the razor in her other hand, and wrapped her fingers around the handle. Then he'd presented his wrist. *"I give you my life. To prove I'm so sorry, to prove that I wish things had turned out different. To prove...I love you."*

I love you.

He tugged his sleeve higher. *"God's Word says there is no greater love than this: that a man would lay down his life for a friend."* He put her hand and the razor to his own flesh. *"If you can't forgive me, if you don't believe I'm a different man, know this."* He leaned forward. *"I love you. He loves you. He gave His life for you. I give my life to you."*

He *had* changed. Because of his relationship with Christ.

Couldn't she?

"Mighty deep thoughts," Toby said softly.

Victoria had been completely lost in the memory. Somehow, they'd strolled all the way down to Boot Hill. The last place she wanted to be. A cemetery.

Toby cleared his throat. "We should turn around. GW said he wouldn't be long."

The memory of her attempted suicide and Logan's sacrificial love had left her wrung out. He'd had such peace, especially at the end. The very end. He'd told her she could have that kind of peace.

"Seems like I recall you used to talk more."

Toby was trying to draw her out. Next to strolling through a cemetery, though, talking wasn't at the top of her list either. "I'm sorry. I was thinking..."

"About those men at the newspaper?"

And the one man who wasn't anything like them. "About all of it."

"Can I ask you something?"

She shrugged, neither giving him a yea nor a nay.

He took it as a yea. "What made you hire that fella to blow up the mine?"

Hurt feelings. "Spitefulness. Vengeance." Oh, God, how meaningless it all was. Vying for power in a worthless, hard-scrabble kingdom nobody would even remember in a hundred years. "Something I thought I owned had been stolen from me, and I wanted to pay the thieves back. It's pointless to say now, but I didn't mean for anyone to die."

"The man you hired to do it, I read he died."

"Yes."

"The newspapers are pretty much calling for your head. How'd you get off...?"

"Get off scot-free?"

He nodded.

"The marshal asked me to leave to spare the town a trial. Honestly, I think he was in as much shock as everyone else. The man who had lit the fuse—the actual murderer—was dead. I just wanted to run before the weight of what I'd done crushed me."

As it threatened to do every second her heart kept beating.

"The marshal showed you mercy."

"He should've hung me."

"You don't sound like you appreciate the favor he did you."

"It was no favor. He determined my sentence. He left me to live with what I'd done."

"Then live. Don't walk around like you're dead on the inside."

"I am. I must be the most vile, worthless thing God ever put on this planet."

Toby clutched her shoulder and made her look at him. "Don't say that. He saved you for a reason. Every life is worth something."

"Not mine. I've been trouble since I was old enough to bat my eyelashes at a man, adding nothing to this world but misery and depravity. I've never thought about anybody but myself."

"Speaking from experience, Victoria, if you're alive, you need to find a way to forgive yourself. If you don't get some peace, this will eat you up inside."

His sage advice from such a young mind led her to wonder about his story. "What did you do, Toby?"

"Killed a man in Abilene."

"Just one?" she unintentionally mocked.

"He was my father."

Victoria let out a soft breath, but found she couldn't judge him or jump to conclusions. They started strolling again.

"I was almost eighteen. Pa went into North Fork to buy supplies. Left me in charge. He was supposed to be gone for a week, but drank up the money in two days." He sighed as if saying there was no way around the truth of it. "Ma was pregnant. He came home and started beating on her, blaming her for the mess his life was. I couldn't watch it anymore. When he threw her up against the fireplace, I swung my rifle at him." He grimaced. "Cracked his skull wide open. Ma went into labor and died. Lost the twins. In one argument, I lost my whole family."

"I'm sorry." And she was. She could understand his pain, his guilt, and she wouldn't wish the feelings on her worst enemies. A new thought for her.

"I served my time in Leavenworth." He rolled his shoulders. "Fella tried to kill me over some oatmeal." He raised his eyebrows as if he still couldn't believe it. "Oatmeal. I got paroled after three years. GW gave me a job. I started working with the horses on his place and discovered I had a gift for helping the worst ones." He slapped his fingers on his thigh. "And it might be hard for you to understand this, but I also surrendered my burdens to Christ. As bad as my pointless, shattered life was, GW explained Jesus could heal me, give me peace and purpose. And He did."

"You sound like Logan." Victoria's throat tightened up on her and she feared she might actually cry here on the street.

"Logan. He was someone special to you?"

"Very. Can we please stop talking now?"

∽

"You're pressing *our* luck by hanging around Dodge." Charlie dealt cards to Lawrence and Oscar with quick, efficient flips. "Even the outskirts of town is too close."

Lawrence raked his cards together and pulled them to his chest. "It'll be good enough. We won't be here much longer." The rough, smoky saloon was way off the main rut in Dodge and offered some anonymity. "I know one thing. No old man with a lady's gun is gonna run me out of town."

Oscar grunted, cards in his hands. "We gotta settle it with him and her at the same time. Easier that way."

"If you're gonna do it," Charlie said, setting down the deck and picking up his own hand, "You'd better do it quick and then run like a scalded dog. Earp will be on you like maggots on a carcass. But you couldn't get the drop on an old man. Not sure I got any confidence you'll be able to get the girl."

Oscar glared at him across the faded felt, the weak lamp swinging overhead adding a cadaverous green tint to his skin. "You need to keep your mouth shut and your opinions to yourself."

Charlie leaned back, dragging his cards with him. "Just sayin', you boys ain't having too much luck getting vengeance for your little brother." He casually sorted his cards as he talked, "Now, me, if I was out for vengeance, I'd be a whole lot smarter than you flunkies."

Lawrence slapped the table, collapsing stacks of chips and drawing the eyes of the few other customers. "You just shut up, you hear? You didn't lose anybody in that mine. We did. It's all her doing and she'll pay for it. Come hell or high water, we'll make Delilah Goodnight pay. When the time is right."

Charlie waved a hand in a gesture of apology. "You're right. That was heartless of me. My apologies. I'm sure you'll make up for your brother's murder, no matter what old man is standing in your way."

The sarcasm sent the normally reserved Lawrence to his feet. "Let me tell you something, Charlie," he growled through clenched teeth. "Nobody is standing in our way. Not you, not Earp, and especially not some old man."

Thirteen

"WHAT'S it like to have a daughter that has so deeply disappointed you?"

The question froze Eleanor as she reached for a piece of chicken. "I don't know." She picked up a leg and set it on her plate. "I don't have one."

Victoria smiled. Eleanor was a wonderful woman but a terrible liar. "You don't have to pretend. I'm trying to understand...what I look like through other people's eyes. Why those men are after me. The pain I've put them—and you—through."

Eleanor sighed, dropped her hands into her lap, and stared at her plate. "All right, I won't lie. It came as quite a shock. I've worked at Big Mike's since you left. I've heard the stories. Things you've done, things that happened in your establishments. And I thought anyone in charge of that had to be pure evil."

Victoria winced.

"But now," Eleanor continued, looking up at her daughter. "Now I understand. You were raging against the world." She reached across their wobbly little table and took her daughter's hand. "Like that horse out at GW's. Just raging. Wondering why the world kept treating you so cruelly. You thought your mother had sold you into prostitution. You thought Logan had forgotten you. I would have hated the world, too. Or at least been sure it hated me."

Yes, Victoria agreed. That about summed it up. Hate. Hate. And more hate. "A better person would have risen above the circumstances."

"You were seventeen. You didn't know any better. You only knew what I'd shown ya."

"Logan tried to tell me about God."

"Who would have ever thought that boy would come to know Jesus?" Eleanor shook her head and pulled back. "Was it for real?"

"Yes." If not for Victoria tempting him at his weakest points, Logan would have been the most perfect, most upstanding Christian man she'd ever met. And even in his failing, he'd found his way back to the Lord.

Her eyes burned from the forming tears, and she blinked them back. Sniffling, she wondered if the pain would ever quit. "His last words to me, he asked me to give God a chance. Let Him be my friend."

Eleanor aimlessly drifted her fork through her green beans, then nodded. "We could..." She licked her lips, "We could go to church Sunday. You and me. If you were of a mind to try things out. God, I mean."

It sounded strange. Trying on God. As if He were a new dress or a robe. But the thought of wrapping herself in His love, in His peace—well, Logan had made God sound so inviting, so *forgiving*. Maybe...maybe. "Yes, Momma, maybe we will."

And maybe tonight, she'd pick up the Bible.

~

Victoria held her breath and clutched the top rail on the corral fence. Toby moved with glacial speed, slowly, slowly, raising his hand to Delilah's nose. Would she stand still? Would she take the caress, or was this a ploy? Would she suddenly rise up on her hind legs, intent on swinging her hooves and crushing Toby's skull?

His eyes were locked with Delilah's. She snorted. Shook her head. Still, he continued raising his hand so slowly that the movement was almost imperceptible. Victoria could hear her blood thrumming in her veins.

Trust him, Delilah. He won't hurt you.

Finally, a mere inch separated Toby's fingers from the horse's nose. His hand hovered. Delilah exhaled noisily but didn't back away. The moment of truth. Toby touched her nose. Touched it again.

The tension broke. Victoria breathed. Toby stroked Delilah's nose twice more, then stepped away and showed her his back. Victoria didn't understand this dance. It required a patience she couldn't fathom.

He casually took two more steps and stopped. Delilah quivered, as if she wanted to follow, but couldn't find the courage within herself.

Come on, girl. Come on. Victoria couldn't explain her sense of desperation for the horse. To hope. To believe. To trust.

Suddenly, Delilah raised a hoof, hovered it indecisively, then moved it forward and set it down. A half-step toward Toby. He winked at Victoria but didn't speak. She was stunned by this feeling of hope—and excitement. The horse had turned a corner. She was beginning to trust Toby.

A little. Fear getting the better of her, Delilah retreated to the far end of the corral and snorted. Toby moseyed on over to

Victoria, a sheepish grin on his face. "That'll have to do for today."

"You must have the patience of Job."

"Sometimes that's what it takes. With horses and people."

His words were aimed at her, but she wasn't ready for even a half-step toward anyone, much less a man.

"The fact is, man is a reeking mass of corruption."

Victoria gaped in surprise at gray-bearded preacher Jim Killian's observation from the pulpit. But also acknowledged how right he was, considering the things she'd seen and done.

"His whole soul is," he continued, "by nature, so debased and so depraved, that no description which can be given of him even by inspired tongues can fully tell how base and vile a thing he is."

Debased and depraved. She surveyed the congregation. Surely no one in this church was as bad a sinner as—

Cooley, GW's fired editor, stared up at the preacher. As if feeling her eyes on him, he cast a quick, dark, sidelong glance her way. Recognition and something darker—hunger, hatred— unveiled themselves, but he turned away quickly.

He has the gall to come to church—

Victoria's arrogance evaporated almost instantly. She was here, too. Surely she was a worse sinner than Cooley.

"Until I know how really and essentially vicious my nature has become, it cannot be possible for me to know the whole extent of my guilt."

Victoria whipped her head back to the preacher. *Oh, no, I know, preacher. I do.*

"We as humans must come to an understanding of how

unholy, ungodly, and depraved we are before we can even begin to understand our need for a Savior."

She had at least achieved that. Victoria Patterson had a crystal clear picture of just how vile a thing she was—

"And then we crave God. We crave forgiveness. We crave a love that washes away, forgets about, casts into the deep, our sins. Allows us to start fresh, freed from the burdensome, choking chains of our past."

Oh, yes, how she craved that. Desperately.

Inexplicably, Victoria's heart started pounding like a terrified deer's. Her breaths came in short, frantic bursts. Her throat constricted. She'd give anything to have her past wiped away. To know God cared and would free her from this guilt.

"My beloved brothers and sisters, God sees us as we are. He sees the sins that made us what we are. More importantly, He also sees us as He made us *to be*: blameless, spotless, and redeemed. By the blood of His son, we can be washed clean. Greed, envy, lust, vengeance, even murder—no sin—NO sin— has moved you past God's reach. There is no place you can hide from His love."

The preacher stepped down from the pulpit and stood in front of it. His arms limp at his sides, he spoke gently. "Are you so burdened by your mistakes you can barely breathe from the weight of them?"

Yes.

"Do you cry out for peace in the middle of the night?"

Yes.

"Does your soul writhe in pain over the choices you've made?"

Yes.

"Come to the cross and lay your burdens down. Christ is waiting to forgive you."

Desperate for peace, Victoria's resistance, her fears, her

walls, all collapsed. She needed Christ more than she needed air in her lungs. The congregation disappeared in her blur of tears as she rose to her feet. The preacher's face transformed with a glow and he extended his hand...

On the buggy ride home, Victoria swung her head every which way. It seemed the world around her was new and different. The fall grass was greener, fresher. The sky was bluer, the air sweeter.

Her heart freer.

She wanted to fling out her arms and spin and spin until she fell down, dizzy with relief.

No, not relief. Joy. She was loved by Someone who knew her darkest secrets, and They did not stop, or even hinder the love.

She'd feared in her soul, down deep where she never wanted to look, that her evil deeds would send her to hell. That fear was gone.

I feel like I can breathe again, Lord. I feel the love Logan told me about. Your love...Your presence in my life. In spite of everything I did, You love me.

The thought was breathtaking. Chains had fallen from her heart, but there was still something...something missing?

"Are you all right," her mother asked. "One minute, you look like you could skip home, and the next..."

"I feel so much better, Momma. Truly like a burden has been lifted from me."

"But...?"

"I'm not sure. I can't find the words. Something left unsaid or undone..."

"Preacher invited us to his Bible study. You gonna go?"

"Yes."

"Maybe the more you learn the easier the answers will come."

"Maybe." Victoria hooked arms with Eleanor, careful not to interfere with her driving, but so happy to have come home.

"I was proud of you walking the aisle like you did. I thought my heart would burst."

"What about you, Momma? Do you believe?"

Eleanor chuckled. "I believed everything I'd ever heard about the Lord the moment you came home. But when you walked to the altar—oh, yes, I gave Him all my heart at that moment." She put the reins in one hand and patted Victoria's knee with the other. "So blessed, so grateful—" Her voice broke and she turned back to the road ahead.

Victoria considered the words. Blessed. Grateful. She would add *contented*. Perhaps it wouldn't last, but at this very moment, with her mother beside her, Victoria could claim a level of contentment she couldn't remember ever feeling.

Eleanor cleared her throat, perhaps chasing away the knot in it. "Thanksgiving is in a few weeks. GW wants us to celebrate with him. I always eat with him, but this year is special. I am truly, deeply thankful."

For the first time in a long time, so was Victoria. "I'll help you cook. I haven't cooked much of anything in a long, long time. You'll have to teach me again."

At first, Eleanor looked pained by the idea, but she nodded and sniffed away a tear. "You have no idea how happy that would make me."

Fourteen

VISITS to the newspaper office did not get any easier for Victoria. The civil talk but cold looks from Jenny and Bobby said they thought they knew her kind so well. How little they actually knew.

Forgiveness, though, was supposed to become a part of her now. Pastor Jim had been pounding this point in the Wednesday Bible study, but, oh, so much easier said than done. Nothing about following Christ came naturally to Victoria.

She pulled the wagon to a stop in front of the paper and wondered if it did for anyone.

GW tugged his sheepskin coat closer and hunched his shoulders against the weather. "The colder it gets, the longer the trip into town gets. Brrrr."

"Feels like it's going to be a cold winter," Victoria said, setting the brake.

"I'll make this quick, so we can dally over some coffee from the café. Oh—" He snapped his fingers. "After we're done here, we need to stop by the hotel. Got a cattle-buyer coming into town. I want to make sure his room is ready."

"All right."

The conversations were quick and perfunctory at the newspaper as GW, Victoria, and Bobby gathered around the press. Cooley had replaced the missing money and quietly resigned. Editor now for only a week, Bobby was proving to be a capable editor, even at his young age, and GW was pleased with the boy.

Victoria read his list of suggested stories aloud but paused before stating the last one. She glanced up at Bobby. He shrugged as if saying *it's news.*

"What?" GW asked, thumping his cane.

"Apparently Cooley is opening his own paper."

"It's confirmed," Bobby said. "He's rented space and got a press ordered."

"Hmmm. I hear his drinking is getting worse, though." GW rested his hands on his hips and worried his bottom lip. "Nah, I doubt he'll be much competition. You up for it, Bobby, if it happens to come about?"

"I think so, sir."

"Good enough. I'm liable to have him arrested before he publishes his first edition anyhow. Once I can prove his embezzling, he'll make an interesting front-page story for us. So"— GW nodded at Victoria—"I reckon we're done here. Let's get to the hotel."

The Dodge House was only one building over. Hand on his elbow, Victoria guided GW down the boardwalk, wincing at the chilly November breeze. As she reached for the door, Charlie pulled it open from the other side. Something flashed in his dark eyes when he saw her, but it vanished before Victoria could identify it. Simple recognition? Embarrassment over their initial meeting?

Reasonable, but she didn't think so.

He pushed a hand through his stringy hair and dropped his

hat in place. "Ma'am. Sir." He stepped back and held the door for them.

"You staying outta trouble, son?" GW asked, a skeptical lift in his brow.

"Oh, yes, sir," Charlie promised. "And my friends are nowhere in town."

"Well, good then." GW dismissed the man with a nod, as did Victoria, and the pair shuffled past him to the desk. The young girl behind it watched Charlie slip out, a dreamy expression on her face.

No accounting for taste, Victoria thought, mystified by the evident attraction.

"My sight may be fading, young lady, but I can still spot cow eyes a mile away. Your pa approve of him?" GW smacked the counter loudly when the girl didn't acknowledge him immediately.

She blinked and straightened up. "Approve? Well...he hasn't exactly met him, only heard about him. But Charlie's mostly staying away from those troublemakers."

"Mostly?"

"They're camped on the edge of town somewhere. I know he's at least checked on them once or twice, but they're staying out of Dodge like they said they would."

Immediately, Victoria wondered why they hadn't headed back to Defiance. Wasn't that the last they'd said? Why would they be hanging around? Her gaze drifted to the window and she was surprised to see Charlie conversing with Cooley. Her lip curled a little. How would they know each other? Their seeming familiarity with each other bothered her.

Probably just met at the saloon, playing cards. You're being paranoid.

"Victoria?"

She returned to GW and the clerk and realized they were both staring at her. "What? I'm sorry."

"Cooper said he wanted a suite. Isn't that what the telegram said?"

"Yes." Her stare drifted back to Charlie and Cooley. "A suite. Preferably overlooking the street."

"That's what we have him down for, GW," the little clerk said.

"All right. He'll be in on the morning train. Thank you, Megan."

"Thank you, GW."

"All right, 'fess up," he said to Victoria as they strolled out of the hotel. "Where was your mind?"

She looked up and down the boardwalk. "I saw Charlie talking to Cooley. Did you notice she said his friends haven't left? They're hanging around the edge of town."

"Yeah, I heard that." He shrugged a shoulder. "Probably just waiting on Charlie to finish wasting time on Megan."

"Probably." But they'd come looking for Delilah Goodnight.

"So, we got any more errands?"

Victoria was willing to tuck away her concerns for the moment. "Just the coffee from the café. Maybe a piece of pie."

"You know, I look forward to your momma's peach cobbler every year at Thanksgiving." The old man patted his stomach. "I've tried to hire her to cook for me twenty times or more, but she never did want to leave town."

Was she afraid she might miss Victoria? "How long have you two known each other?"

GW's old, grizzled face softened. "I came to Dodge right after—" He bit something back, sucked in his bottom lip as if physically keeping down a thought.

"What?"

He swiped a hand over a haggard expression. "Right after she put you on that stage to Stillwater."

Victoria wilted a little. "A fateful decision."

"I reckon." They walked another few feet in silence, but the dip in his brow, the tightness in his jaw, and the more distinct tap of his cane said GW had something on his mind. "I knew your father," he finally said. "You never met him, did you?"

"Nope. Far as I know, he never sent a picture or a letter, nothing. He left Eleanor with me and never came back."

GW sighed, a heavy, burdened sound. "He was my brother."

"Your bro—" Victoria tugged him to a stop and looked up at him, stunned at how the weight of the confession impacted him physically—dulled his eyes, dragged down his normally light expression. "My father was your brother? That makes you my—"

"Uncle."

Taken aback, she couldn't move for a moment and GW shifted forward to get her walking again. "He wrote me and told me the situation. Said he was gonna leave. I urged him not to. I understand he stayed till you were born—"

"Then slipped away one night like a stinking, scared coyote and never came back."

GW flinched at her tone. "Yes, Thomas was a coward. No two ways about it."

"Why did you come here?"

He shrugged. "I was a Texas Ranger for over thirty years. I retired and came here because you and Eleanor were the only family I had. It's a pretty weak thread that connects us, I guess, but it was all I had."

Victoria had never felt the need to be surrounded by friends or family. She'd spent most of her life considering people pawns, and relationships with them as entanglements. She felt differently now. She was feeling differently about a lot of things. *Jesus, will You keep changing me like this, until I have Logan's faith and Toby's peace?*

"I guess I should tell you your pa's dead. Got shot at Fort Sumner. Poker game gone wrong, I heard."

Victoria was not sorry, and she wondered if the Lord would forgive her cold heart. She wasn't angry. She didn't hate her father. She merely couldn't bring herself to care about someone she'd never met. Someday, maybe she would.

She stopped walking as if she'd encountered a wall.

Is that how Elise will think of me? A stranger. Someone who didn't care enough to be a part of her life?

"Victoria?" GW peered at her questioningly.

She had given Elise to a good family to protect her. She couldn't be associated with Delilah Goodnight, not in any way, shape, or form. She could never know the story. At least, not all of it. Logan deserved to be remembered. He was a hero. Maybe someday she would have a chance to talk to her daughter and tell her...a few carefully chosen details.

Victoria shook off the unexpected melancholy. "I was just thinking of someone I might write a letter to. One day." She cheered up for his benefit and to force away his curiosity. "Let's get on to the café."

~

GW admitted to needing a nap after the morning's work and drifted off in front of his fireplace. Victoria stared at him a moment, the snow-white hair, bushy mustache, weathered skin.

Her uncle.

She wondered if her life would have been better if he'd been her father. GW was not a man who ran from anything, especially responsibility.

Puzzled at the direction of her woolgathering, she plucked a crocheted throw from the settee, laid it across his lap, and stopped suddenly. She looked at GW, then down at her own hands in the act of tenderly tucking it in around him. She couldn't recall the last time she'd done a kind gesture for someone other than Eleanor. Even her first offer to do the dishes one night in their new home had been born of duty, because Victoria wasn't lazy. And tending to Toby had been born of necessity.

But this was different. She'd done something nice, something tender...merely because she liked the old man. Maybe Delilah Goodnight really was dead. Not just the persona but the person. What was that scripture the preacher had talked about the other day? Something about being in Christ, old things are passed away. But she did remember the end of it: *Behold, all things are become new.* She liked that and promised to look up the scripture when she got home.

Touching the top of GW's head lightly, she turned and headed for the corral.

Fifteen

DELILAH PADDED NERVOUSLY AROUND TOBY, who stood in the center of the corral with a bridle in his hand.

Tack, Victoria noted. *That's a new step.*

The cool breeze ruffled strands of his blond hair as he adjusted his hat, pressing it a little lower. "Come on girl," he said softly. "We're friends. You can trust me."

Absently wishing she'd worn her coat out here, Victoria shrugged her shoulders against the cold. "The bridle frightens her."

Toby nodded but didn't respond. She had learned he was not being rude. He was watching the horse intently, studying her, learning how to reach her. He had told Victoria during an earlier lesson that he didn't mind conversation if she didn't expect immediate answers.

"Do you think she knows what it is?"

"I think she knows exactly what it is." Toby flexed gloved fingers as if they were cold. "She knows she can trust me, but now she has to surrender. Speaking of which, I was in church Sunday."

A blush warmed Victoria's cheeks. So he'd seen. She was not ashamed of what she'd done. On the contrary, her run to the altar had changed her life. She just wasn't quite sure *how* yet, and she didn't know what to say about things. "I..." She clutched the top rail and drummed her fingers. "I'm happy. For the first time in years, but I don't quite know what to do, or how this plays out. How to walk with Him."

"Well..." He trailed off, seemed to think about her comment for a moment. Rubbing his chin, he slowly spun around to face her. "You're a lot like this horse here." A cockeyed smile toyed with his lips. "You've put your trust in someone other than yourself. But you both need to learn to surrender. She'll learn it through bit and bridle and a gentle hand. You'll learn it through reading His word."

"I bet He has His own bit and bridle."

"It doesn't have to be a battle, Victoria."

Toby strode over to face her, his face, his whole being, glowing with excitement. An unexpected desire to touch his stubbly chin or drift her fingers over his dirt-smudged cheek surprised her into stepping back from the fence.

"He wants to guide you. Just like I want to guide Delilah there. If you can get it in your head that He wants what's best for you, you'll go along willingly."

God wants what's best for me. I need to trust that. Believe it. "That's the surrender you've been talking about."

"Yeah. No broken spirits. Lifted ones."

She looked down at her hands clenched at her waist, a bit blue from the cold. "Yes, I'm tired of the broken ones."

～

Toby reached through the fence and lifted Victoria's chin. He stared into her magical amber eyes and smiled at the difference he saw now. They were brighter, warmer, more vibrant. Wisps of her auburn hair, caught in the breeze, flitted around the edges of her face, and he pushed a strand back. "You were pretty before, but the Man you're walking with now makes you glow. Feels good to have some of that weight off your shoulders, doesn't it?"

"Yes, it does. I can't remember the last time I felt so..." She frowned, seemed to search for the right sentiment. "Light. You're right, it is a weight that's gone. Or mostly gone. And the idea of surrender doesn't scare me anymore."

It wasn't the time, but Toby's mouth jumped ahead of his brain. "Victoria, you wouldn't want...?" He cocked his head a little and flinched. This was a stupid idea, but he'd started. So... "You wouldn't want to go to dinner with me sometime, would you?"

She moved away from him and plucked at a splinter poking up from the top rail. "We eat dinner with you all the time."

"No, I mean..." He lowered his head a little to peer at her, trying to get her to look at him. "Just the two of us. Just you and me." Her hand stopped its fidgeting. Her expression fell, saddened. He straightened up. "Guess that's a no, huh?"

"It's not you. I still can't—I am—" She exhaled a long breath. "I still hurt too much to think about another man."

He drummed leather-covered fingers on the fence. Competing with a dead man. Well, death and grief had to run their courses. "I understand. I'm sorry—"

"No, don't apologize. Your heart is still in the land of the living. Nothing wrong with that. Mine might be someday."

"I'm a patient man. You said it yourself."

And he resigned himself to the wait.

Sixteen

WITH HER UNHOLY and decadent past, Victoria wouldn't have thought it possible she could be shopping for a Thanksgiving meal like any other church-going, Dodge City resident. Part of her thought it was a joke—the part that tried to condemn her for attempting to change.

But she *had* changed.

God had cleared her debts and was working on her conscience. She would never stop grieving over the deaths of Logan or all those men in the mine, but God knew she was sorry—truly, deeply remorseful. And, inexplicably, knowing He'd forgiven her made their deaths easier to bear.

Smiling to herself, she stepped out on the boardwalk with the first box of groceries. "GW, I've got—"

The bench right in front of the store was empty. A sudden, sinking feeling hit her. She scanned the walk in both directions, then the street. The buggy was gone as well. The old fool couldn't drive. Where would he go—?

"If you're looking for GW, he left."

Victoria rounded on Cooley. He came sauntering down the

way, spinning an oak cane like he was the Duke of Sussex, a leer pasted on his bony face.

"What do you mean, he left? He can't drive."

"I saw him and that fella Charlie jump in the buggy and take off in a hurry."

"Where were they going?"

His eyebrows shot up. "I have no idea. He asked if the old man was with you, and I told him yes." A cool smile lifted his lips. "My first issue is only days away. I bet you can guess my front-page story."

She didn't have time for this. "Are you sure you don't know where they were going?"

He ignored her. "It's quite the news—one of the West's most decadent madams living in Dodge City. Did you really think this was the best place to hide your past?" He paused. "And the deaths in Defiance?"

For an instant, Victoria's mind reeled and she wanted to claw out the man's eyes. She bit down on her tongue and prayed. In fact, she was surprised at how naturally the cry for help rose to her mind. *Please, Father, make him go away*—

"Well"—the grin melted off Cooley's face—"I'll be back in touch, *Miss Patterson*," he mocked.

She, however, wasn't the issue right now. "Which way did they go?"

He stopped, half-turned. "Who?"

"GW and Charlie?"

"Oh, east." He pointed with his cane. "Out of town."

Victoria scanned the busy street. Bit by bit, she pieced things together. Oscar and Lawrence had come here to find her and, thanks probably to a tip from Cooley, had tracked her down at the newspaper. GW and Earp had supposedly run them out of town, so why hang around? Were they waiting for Charlie...or Victoria?

Or GW?

Cooley had to know GW would be coming after him over the financial mismanagement at the paper. Was it a motive to harm the old man?

Had the smarmy newspaper editor convinced vigilantes who were here for Delilah Goodnight to work for him?

Either way, that foolish, lovable old fart was in trouble. Without worrying about her groceries, Victoria dropped them on the bench and raced off to the marshal's office—only to find it empty. Earp was out on his rounds, apparently. Oh, if only Toby were here.

But he's not. Slapping the doorpost in anger, a little of the old Delilah reared her head. *Get a buggy and go find GW. If they want you and not him, make the trade. He's worth more to this town than you are.*

Not arguing with the sentiment, she headed back to Eleanor's. Someone needed to know where she was going. Maybe her mother could find Earp and he'd send help.

Only Eleanor wasn't home either. An open canister of flour sat out on the counter. Pie crusts had been rolled out and abandoned. A single, hardy fly buzzed around a bowl of sliced peaches.

Fear wiggling in her gut, Victoria called out. "Eleanor?" The silence was solid and suffocating. "Momma?" Her voice broke at the end of the word and her thoughts rocketed back to Lawrence and Oscar. Had GW and Eleanor been taken together?

The awful possibilities galvanized her feet and she was running to the livery like the world was coming to an end. Heart pounding, she grabbed a young boy by the collar who was cleaning a stall. "I need something to ride, right now."

Eyes bulging, red hair spilling over his freckled cheeks, he backpedaled to get away from the crazy woman. "Wha—what can I do for ya, ma'am?"

"I need to ride or drive something right now." She backed up a step to keep the child from panic. "I don't care. Anything."

"I'll have a horse saddled for ya in a jif."

"Faster," she commanded. *Please, God, faster...*

But she really meant, *don't let it be too late.*

"Find Marshal Earp," she said as the boy handed over a sorrel. "Tell him—" Tell him what? She didn't know where she was going. "Tell him GW might be in trouble." She swung up into the saddle, her skirt bunching up on the horse's rump and exposing a scandalous amount of her calf. "But I don't know where he is. He'll have to look. Somewhere on the edge of town, I think." *God, please let that be right.* "Tell him, you hear?"

The boy backed away as she kicked the horse. "Yes, ma'am."

Skirt flapping around her knees, whipping out behind her, Victoria galloped out of town, uncaring of the curious stares. Panic clawed at her throat. She couldn't think of anything the girl at the hotel or Charlie or even Cooley had said that was a specific clue. *Oh, God, lead me, please,* she prayed. *Don't let anyone else die because of me.*

She raced toward the end of town, past Boot Hill, out on to the vast, open prairie. A gray, angry sky overhead reflected her torment. Frustrated, confused, she slowed her horse from a gallop to a canter to a trot...finally to a standstill.

The wind whistled. Dry, amber grass danced and swayed around her. A few cottonwoods stood silently nearby, their shadows growing long in the late afternoon sun. She thought back to her early days here, when innocence and youth fed her hopes and dreams. Places she and Logan had gone to...to be alone.

The memory of a favorite place surfaced.

Benton's Gulch.

Did the sod shanty still stand down by Crier's Sink Hole? It was a fine hiding place.

She scanned the empty prairie.

And a good ride.

Twilight was quickly giving way to night. She wasn't sure she could make it before full dark. If she couldn't? Could she find the old meeting place?

There was no debate here. This was foolish, going in without any help or even a gun. But she had to try. At least scout out the situation then return to town to find Earp or Toby or someone.

Victoria turned the horse west and raced the dying light. She rode hard as the sky melted from reds and oranges into purple. On the verge of black, the evening star blinking alone in the darkness, she reached the bottom of a long, low hill. She squinted, looking for a shape.

If this it, Lord, there should be an old—

Grave.

She dismounted and stumbled in the dark toward a shape, the horse in tow. She nearly tripped over the catawampus wrought-iron fence that surrounded the looming tombstone. Confident of her location, she loosely tied the horse to the tip of a spire. A tumbleweed blew into his rear legs and he nearly spooked free. Shushing him, Victoria tied him again, praying he didn't jerk free from the decrepit thing. Satisfied he'd stay, she crept toward the crest of the hill.

The Kansas prairie, much like an ocean, hid secrets between the swells. Near the top of the rise, she lay down on her stomach and peered through the grass. Below, figures moved about in the firelight, some hovering over the flames, a few sitting on the edge of the light. Wind rippled the water that filled the deep sinkhole. A man in dark clothes stood in the doorway of the dilapidated and collapsing sod house. A rush of sweet memories took Victoria back to seventeen, riding out here with Logan, kissing in that very entrance beneath a fat harvest moon... swearing their eternal love.

Pain twisted in her heart. They both had lost so much. So much. She softly cleared her throat and tried to focus. Eleanor and GW sat by the fire. That was Charlie in the doorway. The two men who had accosted her at the newspaper—Oscar and Lawrence—that was probably them sitting on their bedrolls, watching their hostages.

From this distance, the wind scattered their voices to the prairie. She'd have to get closer. Scanning the hillside below, she saw a rock outcropping—not big—barely larger than a horse, but it would do. She would slink down to it. If things fell apart, she had enough of a lead to get back to her horse and go for help. She scanned the hill behind her. At least, she was fairly sure in the dark she could make it.

Seventeen

SITTING HUNKERED down in the grass, trying to dredge up her courage, Victoria lamented her thin coat. If she'd grabbed her heavy wool frock, perhaps she wouldn't feel so cold, so stiff. Or was that just fear?

Flipping up the collar on the canvas jacket, she quietly slipped through the darkness and the dry grass toward the rock outcropping. Only a few feet lower, yet the wind died suddenly here, and she could hear the snapping fire, neighing horses, and Charlie's voice.

"She'll be along. Any time now, I suspect."

"What makes you so sure she'll find us?" Lawrence said.

Victoria crawled carefully down to the rock, flinching at the gravel she disturbed, well-aware sound was carrying easier now.

"The kids have known about this place since I was a boy," Charlie said. "She probably came here. It's where you go when you want to hide."

"I say we go find her." Oscar tilted his head back, taking a swig from a bottle. "You stay here, Charlie, and watch those two."

Lawrence climbed to his feet, swaying a little as he did. "I like that idea. She's probably"—a growling burp escaped him—"alone, moving around, trying to find them."

"She won't come for us," Eleanor said, sounding anxious. "At least not alone. She'll find Earp."

"Or Toby," GW added.

"Earp's busy," Charlie said. "He's on a wild goose chase over toward Cimarron."

Lawrence tilted his head. "That was a good idea. Why'd you do that? I thought you didn't want no part in hunting Delilah."

"She'll bring Toby," GW said somberly. "He won't just hand her over."

"Yeah, maybe," Charlie said brightly. "But I think she'll waste so much time looking for Earp, she'll decide she don't have time to ride out to the ranch. I'm betting she comes after you two. Alone."

Charlie straightened and stepped outside the doorway. "I guess it's time to wrap all this up. Besides, it's getting cold." Without any warning, he drew his revolver and shot Lawrence in the head, and before the man hit the ground, Charlie dropped Oscar. The fire from his barrel illuminated GW and Eleanor surging to their feet as Victoria screamed.

The echo of the shots and her shrill cry faded together, but all eyes turned up the hill to her. Misery writhed in Victoria's chest. She pushed herself out from behind the rock. "Stop it!" Tears choked her voice. "For God's sake, just stop it." *More death on account of me. Oh, God, am I cursed? Please stop all this.* "Why did you do that?" she screamed, nearly hysterical.

"Come down here and we'll talk about it, *Victoria*."

Charlie said her name like it was a huge joke. Bitterness, rage, grief, strangled her. She pressed her fists to her temples. "So, this *is* about me. Oh, God, oh, God," she whispered. "This has to stop." She stared up at the night sky, slowly coming to life with sparkling diamonds, and wrangled control back into her voice. "You lose someone in Defiance?"

"You could say that."

"Run, Victoria," Eleanor screamed, stepping forward. "Run."

"Shut up, old woman!" Charlie cocked his revolver. "Or I'll shoot you, too."

"No," Victoria screamed, reaching out futilely.

"You do, and I'll kill you," GW said quietly, ominously.

Charlie snorted and lowered the weapon. "You saw how fast I killed Lawrence and Oscar."

"I'm closer."

Victoria's feet were rooted to the ground. GW's comment seemed to rattle Charlie and he took a step back. "Get down here, Victoria. I'll let these two walk away if you do. You leave for the sheriff and I'll kill 'em both."

Her knees buckled, and she clutched the rock. She would trade herself, gladly. She deserved to be murdered, but how could she be sure he'd let GW and Eleanor go? Eleanor had to live. She'd already been through so much.

"Victoriaaaa," Charlie sang mockingly.

"Don't listen to him," GW yelled. "Get out of here. Find Earp." He cast a quick glance at Charlie. "He'll handle this miscreant."

Victoria angrily brushed tears from her cheeks. "Tell me why you're doing this. Why did you kill those two?"

"I don't need 'em anymore."

Victoria's mind raced. Should she run? No, she knew how this had to play out. "Who are you?" she asked, miserable and heartsick. But, oddly, not afraid.

"I'm Charlie Smith. I'm one of the boys Logan used to run with. Long time ago. Kinda hurts my feelings you don't remember me."

Eleanor stuck her chin in the air. "I didn't let her run with Logan once he started hanging about with you."

Charlie scratched his chin. "I remember she disappeared. And Logan changed. Like somebody blowing out a lamp. He got mean, just like that." He snapped his fingers. "Sometimes he was like the wrath of God with that gun hand of his. And sometimes, he was like Samson with a jawbone. A gun or fists, either way, he was a legion of trouble."

"You got a point to this?" GW asked, fury rattling in his voice.

Charlie sagged, paused for a moment, then raised his gun to GW. "My brother took a bullet 'cause of him in Nebraska four years ago. We were trying to rob a stage and Logan was drunker than a rat in a whiskey barrel. Stupid son of a—" The curse was lost in a gust of wind. "He disappeared after that, but I have been on his trail like a bloodhound. Finally, I got wind he was masquerading as a *preacher*," he spat the word, "in Defiance." He raised his voice, apparently to be sure Victoria heard this part. "I showed up right after your two-bit drunk went and killed him. Or that's the way the story's told. But he ain't dead. You know it. And I know it."

"What?" Victoria couldn't believe her ears, though the man sounded serious. "You think Logan's still a—?"

"Alive? I know he's still alive."

"Mister, you're out of your mind." Victoria took two steps toward them. "He died in my arms, in the middle of the street." Her voice rose with hysteria. "He's dead, and he's never coming back."

Charlie shook his head. "You're good, but you ain't convincing. He died and you skedaddled. At first, I thought maybe you two had met up somewhere in Colorado. Then I started hearing the stories. He's working his way here." The fire snapped. "To you."

"What are you talking about?" Could this get any more insane or absurdly cruel? "He's dead," she whispered, barely loud enough for them all to hear. "He's dead, and I'd give any —" She broke off. "Stories? What stories?"

"I lucked out with Lawrence and Oscar there. They could track. They were tracking you. I knew if I found you, I'd eventually find Logan. Sure enough, about the time we realized you were here somewhere in Dodge, I saw the pattern. The stories added up."

Victoria couldn't stop her mind from spinning. She felt faint. "What stories?" she asked again. "What pattern? What are you talking about?"

Charlie paused and tilted his head. "A man in black popped up on the trail a few weeks back. Looking for a pretty girl, maybe named Victoria. Maybe coming from Defiance. Quiet fella, kept his hat pulled down real low. Following the same trail we took.

"One fella in Cheyenne Wells didn't take to the questioning." Charlie's voice took on a distant, dreamy quality, as if he were discussing something holy. "He slapped leather with him. Word is our mystery man jerked his Colt so fast, he made lightning look like molasses."

Victoria felt her heart slow to a crawl. Her head swam. Logan? Alive? She'd sat beside him on his deathbed, held his cold fingers in hers. It wasn't possible...

Was it? God? Is Logan alive?

Eighteen

"YOU THINK...?" Victoria could hardly speak. A maelstrom of emotions raged in her soul. "You think this man in black is Logan and he's coming for me?"

"I get you, I get Logan. He's coming for you like a moth to a flame. Honestly, until I heard he was asking about you, trying to find you, I thought you two had planned to meet up somewhere. But that don't matter now. What does matter is he'll be here. Soon, I think."

Victoria literally couldn't fathom this insanity. Oh, hope sparked in her breast, but she knew what she'd seen. She couldn't let hope catch fire. It would make her go crazy. "I'll trade for Eleanor and GW, but you're too late to get vengeance on Logan. Too late..." her voice faded.

"Get down here and we'll talk or"—he raised the pistol again, pointing it at Eleanor—"I start cutting baggage loose."

"No, Victoria," Eleanor cried.

"Get the marshal," GW ordered.

No. Victoria couldn't stand the thought of coming back to their bodies. Charlie was going to kill them if she didn't play this his way. Probably would anyway. *Oh, God, please, please keep them safe. But I should pay for my crimes.*

She raised her hands into the air. "I'm coming down." Every fiber in her being knew Charlie was going to kill GW and Eleanor. He didn't need them. In his sick, twisted mind, he believed Victoria was the magnet for Logan. If only that could be true.

But Logan was dead. No one was coming to save them. And Charlie was a hair trigger away from delivering more death.

Victoria stumbled down the incline through the tangle of buffalo grass to level ground. Charlie still held the gun on GW and Eleanor. Their only chance lay in a distraction. She prayed they would act when the opportunity arose.

Oh, God, I could get us all killed. Her steps faltered, but something kept her feet moving. She came within twenty feet of Charlie and surveyed Eleanor's and GW's conditions. "Momma, are you all right?"

Her mother nodded and made a choked noise

"GW?"

"You shoulda run. Somebody has to survive this."

"Yes." A peace flooded over Victoria. She knew what she had to do, and her muscles readied for the charge. "Someone will." She would take the bullet, and Eleanor and GW would overpower Charlie.

It would be all right. Accounts would be settled. And for the first time in her life, the ugly face of death didn't frighten her.

The message to move was shooting from her brain to her legs when a shot boomed over their heads from the darkness. Charlie stepped back, waved his gun around, but brought it back quickly to his hostages. Hope surged in Victoria. Earp? Was Earp out there in the grass and shadows?

"Who's out there?" Charlie yelled, his eyes wildly searching the darkness. "I got hostages. I'll drop 'em. Back off!"

The silence was deafening as it stretched out. After a moment, a quiet, calm voice spoke. "So much as blink at them, and I will drop you."

Victoria gasped. Toby? How had he found them?

Charlie's eyes widened. "Who's out there?"

"Drop the gun," Toby ordered again. "I won't repeat myself."

Charlie debated. His gaze bounced back and forth between Victoria and his other two prisoners.

"He's got the drop on you, son," GW said flatly.

A hard thud emanated from the back of Charlie's head and he abruptly slithered to the ground—revealing Toby, his body tight as a pouncing mountain lion, the firelight flickering on the coal black .44 in his right hand. "Next time, don't debate so long."

Eleanor's feet hurt from standing in the kitchen, but her spirit was light as gossamer wings. She sat down at GW's table, the turkey and their favorite foods covering it, and gazed with affection at her old friend. Yes, his brother had been a scoundrel, but if not for GW, Eleanor thought the loneliness might have killed her. He'd helped keep her chin up and her feet rooted in Dodge.

She shifted her attention across the table to Victoria and Toby. Joy surged through her. If Toby hadn't stopped at the livery to pick up some repaired tack, he wouldn't have seen the jittery little stable boy desperate to find Earp. *Oh, thank you, Lord, for Toby and fast horses.* She had to dab at her eyes to squelch the tears. *You told me to be patient and look what you've restored to me.*

"I'll say the blessing." GW put his hands out, and the group entwined their grasps, bowing their heads. "Oh, Heavenly Father, You have truly overwhelmed us this Thanksgiving with the ultimate blessing—life." He paused, and Eleanor guessed he was struggling with a lump in his throat, just as she was. "You snatched us from the jaws of death, and we are exceedingly grateful for Your protection and Your provision. We humbly thank You for restoring Victoria to her mother, but more importantly, for restoring her as Your child. No longer a daughter of defiance, she is a daughter of the King."

A praise of joy nearly escaped Eleanor, but the tears did. *Oh, yes, Father, thank You, thank You.*

"Father," GW continued. "May we live appreciating every breath we take, holding tight every moment we spend with our loved ones, and counting every blessing You grant us with true humility and gratitude. In Your Son's name, we pray." The silence at the table lingered, punctuated by sniffles. GW cleared his throat and grinned at Eleanor. "I've waited all year for this." He extended his hand and motioned to the knife in front of her. "I'll carve."

Victoria agreed with GW's prayer. She wasn't a daughter of defiance anymore, and her soul was light. Freed. Still, this feeling of something...she struggled to define it. Not emptiness. Not sadness. She couldn't stop thinking about the families in Defiance who had been impacted by the mine explosion. But Charlie's words kept trying to drift in, mingle with her thoughts, distract her. There was no way Logan could be alive. She'd been sitting by his bed when he'd taken his last breath. She simply wouldn't allow any hope to take root.

She poked her slice of turkey. Picked up a knife and cut a

bite. As she sampled it, she glanced around the table. Her mother, GW, Toby. What fine people. She was blessed. She was forgiven.

Yet her mind roiled.

Knowing she couldn't get the answers right now, here in the middle of Thanksgiving dinner, she forced her attention to the present company and said a silent prayer of gratitude for them.

Later, after she and Eleanor had cleaned up, Victoria wandered down to the corral to watch Toby work with Delilah. A cool day, the sky overhead was a pristine, flawless sapphire. The November breeze grazed her neck, and she decided she wouldn't stay long, but she liked seeing Delilah's progress.

This time, Victoria was shocked to find Toby actually in the saddle and riding Delilah around the ring. "This seems sudden."

A little wry smile lifted the corner of his mouth as he trotted by her. "She was a good horse before the abuse. Once I got her trust, once she was willing to take the bit in her mouth, she just had to remember her manners."

"Just like that?"

"Sometimes it *is* just like that."

Victoria recalled something she'd read the night before. "And when he came to himself, he said, How many hired servants of my father's have bread enough and to spare, and I perish with hunger!"

"Luke. The prodigal son?"

"When he came to himself," she repeated, more to herself than Toby. "Sometimes, it is just like that. The moment of surrender. Even though the trail to that moment can be mighty long." Her gaze drifted out to the wide, rolling hills past the corral.

Toby gave her a puzzled glance. "Yeah, I suppose so."

Families in misery.

Could Logan be alive?

I should ask their forgiveness.

The last thought made her lungs seize up and she gasped. For a moment, she couldn't breathe. She mentally walked around the idea as if it were a two-headed calf. *Is that it, God? Is that why I keep thinking something isn't quite right? That I've left something undone? A wound open?*

But the thought of going back to Defiance filled her with... Peace.

She exhaled. But what if Logan was alive and he was looking for her? "No, it's not possible," she whispered. She would know if he were alive. No, these were just rumors and tall tales sprouting up around his reputation. Besides, in the cold light of day, nothing mattered more than those families she'd hurt. Could she give them any peace?

It felt right, this idea of facing these people she'd hurt, but she was still afraid.

Oh, God, will I be safe? Or will they lynch me?

Be not afraid. The Lord your God goes with you...

Victoria looked up at GW's back porch. She could see her mother's plump shadow behind the screen. The shadow waved, and Victoria waved back, her heart swelling with thankfulness for the time she'd had with Eleanor.

Oh, momma, I'm sorry to have to leave. I pray she understands, Lord. Please, let her understand. There are sons and daughters in Defiance, too, who have lost loved ones. Maybe I can do something to ease their suffering. Even if it means going to jail.

Victoria didn't have a plan. She didn't know how the town would receive her. Maybe they would stone her. Maybe they would arrest her. Or, just maybe, they would find forgiveness and let it heal them.

Nineteen

TOBY SAT down at the kitchen table alone with the last remaining piece of peach cobbler. GW would kill him, but he'd caught a chill working with Delilah this morning and thought cobbler and coffee would revive him. After a moment of eating in silence, he noticed the odd quiet in the house and it puzzled him.

Victoria and Eleanor had been here the last few days, ever since Thanksgiving. They'd said it was because staying just made clean-up and finishing off leftovers easier, but Toby suspected the three were becoming a family. He took a sip of his coffee and wondered if there was a chance he could be the fourth member.

That fracas on the prairie with Charlie had set a few notions loose in Toby's head—once he'd managed to get his pulse under control. What would he have done if he hadn't gotten there in time? The thought of GW and Eleanor shot dead was bad enough, but Victoria lying there with a bullet in her—no, he couldn't even fathom. Which told him it was time to see if there might be something more here than friendship.

But Victoria was even more skittish than Delilah. He could hardly imagine it, but he would have to go even slower with her. He gulped his last sip of coffee, set his dishes in the sink, and headed back outside. Passing the library, he heard the muffled voices behind the great oak doors. No words, but the tone struck him as somber, troubled.

None of his business, he supposed. Still, a little concerned, he dropped his hat in place and plucked his coat from the hook by the door.

He was in the stall grooming Delilah when Victoria wandered into the barn, all wrapped up in one of GW's sheepskin coats. He couldn't help but smile. She looked like a toddler wearing her father's clothes.

"You can even groom her now?"

She sounded shocked. Toby dragged the curry comb down the horse's back. "Once she made up her mind I'm not out to hurt her, she decided to go back to being the horse she was."

Victoria's brow scrunched. "I don't want to go back. Who I am right now—this"—she struggled for words—"peace that I'm known by Him, through and through, but loved anyway—I don't ever want to give that up."

Toby tossed the brush into a bucket and turned to her. "You won't have to. Nothing will ever separate you from His love." *Or mine.* The thought surprised him.

Again, Victoria's expression changed. Saddened. Her lips tensed. "Toby, I wanted to tell you myself. I'm going to go back to Defiance."

It had been a long time since news had hit him like a sledgehammer. He tried to freeze his face while he absorbed her news but suspected he didn't quite hide his shock or disappointment.

She ambled over to Delilah and haltingly laid a timid hand on her cheek. The horse accepted the touch and Victoria exhaled. "Yes, she's like a different animal."

Thoughts whirled in Toby's mind. Was there nothing he could say to keep her here? He grasped at a mental straw. "Charlie said Logan was on his way here to find you. What if you miss him?"

She shook her head. "Logan's dead. I think people are just trying to create a legend. I wish they'd let him rest in peace." She brightened and forced a smile at him. "Besides, if he shows up, you'll know where I am." Perhaps she saw the pain Toby was trying to mask. Her countenance changed again, to compassion and, worse, pity. "I'm sorry, Toby. You are a good man. If I stayed here, I'm sure I'd fall in love with you."

"Then maybe you should stay." It came out sounding more serious, more desperate than he'd meant for it to but he couldn't take it back now.

Her amber eyes shining with moisture, she caressed his stubbly cheek. "I don't want to think about me first anymore. I've spread around a lot of misery, Toby. I need to see if I can do something good for a change."

Epilogue

DELILAH WAITED QUIETLY in her stall. She grumbled softly when Toby opened the gate and stepped inside with her.

"Let's go show you off, girl." He tried to sound light-hearted but was far from it in truth.

As he saddled Delilah, he dreaded Victoria's imminent departure. He regretted not having had a chance with her, yet he understood things were as they should be. For the time being. Maybe she'd come back.

Maybe he'd head to Defiance.

Eleanor was going with Victoria. GW was pretty down over the departure as well and had told Toby, "They're doing what they think is best. Not our place to interfere right now."

Right now. So maybe later?

He snagged the cinch tight. The idea of leaving glowed a little brighter, but what of GW? *I could use some direction, Lord. Maybe not a burning bush, but something that could point to whether I should or shouldn't go, and when, if I do?*

He swung up into the saddle and trotted a trusting, surrendered Delilah over to the house. He pulled up in front, next to the wagon loaded with trunks and a bed frame. Eleanor and Victoria had stopped to say goodbye.

Toby wished he could skip this part.

Flurries drifted about as he waited for GW to usher his guests outside. Momentarily, the door clicked, and he and the ladies all filed out onto the porch. Victoria's face lit up when she realized the identity of the horse.

She clasped her hands over her chest and shook her head. "You said you could make her a good horse."

Toby took a deep breath, patted Delilah on the neck, and dismounted. "Yeah, she's a fine horse." He pulled the reins over Delilah's head and held them out. "And she's yours."

GW stepped up and dropped a hand on Victoria's shoulder. "I want you to have her."

Her chin quivering, Victoria shuffled down the steps and took the reins but lingered a moment on Toby. "Thank you."

He shoved his hands into his pockets and shrugged. "You two go together. Some things you have to let happen." A puzzled dip formed in her brow, but Toby backed up a step to end the questioning. "Turns out she has a tender mouth. Guide her gently."

A little smile lifted Victoria's lips. "I will."

"Toby..." GW hobbled down the steps, the cane only making the effort slightly easier. "I've been thinking, and Eleanor and I have been talking. Pack some clothes, son, I want you to see these ladies to Defiance."

He felt his eyes widen and he glanced at Victoria. For a moment, she too, looked startled, but the expression faded quickly. She bit down on her bottom lip and smiled warmly. "I think that's an excellent idea. We'll be so much safer with you along." She let her fingers flit quickly down his arm. "Take us to Defiance, Toby."

A Sneak Peek at
Book Five

≈

A DESTINY IN DEFIANCE

Preface

Funny how characters seem to develop minds of their own. When I started this book, Hope Clark was going to be my main protagonist. As the story grew, blossomed, developed, life in Defiance happened to my characters, and the Holy Spirit took me in other directions.

Charles and his rivalry—not just with Matthew—but with his own need for control, rose to the top. How does a good man run a bad town? How does he keep his family safe and their lives peaceful if not by brute force? How does he really let go and trust God for the things he used to get himself?

Aren't these questions for us all?

Hope's story is the biggest sub-plot. You should know, she is based on the historical character of Doc Susie Anderson, a legendary physician who made her way alone in the Rockies. A formidable woman who truly loved her vocation and her patients, she traveled the region, helping the sick and dying. Her story is fascinating, and I include it at the end of *A Destiny in Defiance*.

I hope you enjoy riding into Defiance with me once more. There's a lot going on in town...

God bless and happy reading!

Heather

Just as you don't know
   the way of the wind
   or how bones grow
   in a pregnant woman's womb,
   so you don't know the work of God,
   the maker of everything.

—Ecclesiastes 11:5 (ESV)

One

TICK. Tick. Tick.

Dr. Hope Clark tried to ignore how loudly the Regulator wall clock resonated in her empty office. She surveyed the tiny waiting room, devoid of patients, and sighed. She couldn't go much longer like this. If just one sick person would walk through that door, she felt certain she could win over many, many of the citizens of Denver.

It could all start with one.

As if in answer to prayer, her doorknob turned and slowly the door began to swing open. Hope jolted to attention, touched the stethoscope hanging at her neck to make sure it was still there, and pasted on a smile.

A cumbersome pink hat buried beneath ostrich feathers appeared in the entrance. It led the way for an older, quite rotund woman in a blue velvet dress who peered with suspicion around the room.

"Good morning," Hope said, crossing the room quickly, before the woman could take in the lack of other patients. "I'm Dr. Clark."

She offered her hand, but the woman's eyes narrowed and she pulled back, as if Hope's greeting was offensive. "Yes. I know who you are."

Spirits sagging, Hope tried not to show her disappointment. Somehow, she knew the woman was not here for a health visit. Floundering, she lowered her hand and smiled. "What can I do for you, Miss...?"

"I'm Mrs. Abbington Chalmers. Perhaps you know my husband? The mayor."

"I am not personally acquainted, but I know of him."

Mrs. Chalmers sniffed, as if the answer didn't surprise her. "I am not here, however, on his behalf. I am here on behalf of the Ladies League of Greater Denver."

Lovely, Hope thought. *Not a patient. Worse. She wants a donation.* "Yes. How can I help you?"

For a moment, Mrs. Chalmers' hauteur wavered. The confidence exuded by her raised chin and squared shoulders faded a bit, or so Hope thought. "Well, it isn't easy to say what I've come here for."

"When I have difficult news for my patients, Mrs. Chalmers, I tell them outright. Beating around the bush can be unnecessarily cruel."

That brought the woman's chin back up. "Right you are. So I shan't beat around the bush, as you say. I've come to tell you, Miss Clark, that you have had no patients and you will not have any."

Hope blinked and wondered if she'd heard correctly. "I'm sorry."

Mrs. Chalmers twirled away in a flurry of ostrich feathers and blue velvet, presenting her back. "Women have their place in the world, Miss Clark."

"Doctor," Hope corrected without thinking.

The woman stiffened, slowly turned back to Hope. Her

pudgy face, so round and soft, did not hide the heat in the woman's dull brown eyes, or the disdain in her thinned lips. "I see I need to speak plainly. You upset the balance. Women in Denver and in the rest of the world are happy with their stations in life. We are mothers and caregivers. Helpmeets to our husbands. We run our homes, raise our children, and give our husbands a place to rest from the world. You—"

"Threaten that," Hope interrupted wearily. She had heard all this before but from *men* back in Pennsylvania. The women, for the most part, had been cool and silent regarding her vocation. To hear this nonsense spoken aloud—by a woman—nearly left her speechless. Nearly. "You think I put the idea into your husbands' heads that you're capable of more than birthing babies and hosting cotillions? You prefer the myth that women are the mentally weaker sex. It keeps your credit account at the dress shop open."

Mrs. Chalmers gasped. "How dare you—?"

"With grim purpose and determination is how. I harbor the burning desire to help people, Mrs. Chalmers. I know that I am capable of helping them—possibly even saving their lives—and sitting back on my padded bustle simply will not do."

Mrs. Chalmers snapped her mouth shut and her face flushed. "There are men for that vocation, *Miss* Clark. The letters *M-D* do not make you a doctor."

The verbal slap, so wrong, but so vindictive, stung. Hope knew of course, graduating at the top of her class from Pennsylvania Women's College would mean nothing to this grand dame. Worse, Mrs. Chalmers might see it as a threat, to her way of life, her unchallenged, comfortable existence.

Hope did not want to fight this fight against her own sex. She couldn't believe she had to, especially here in the West where women were reportedly so strong and independent. "I'm sorry you feel this way, Mrs. Chalmers. I strongly believe, however, that women are as cap—"

"You've had no patients." The woman leaned forward a little. "As I said, you will have none. The Ladies League will see to it." Her chin rose higher in triumph. "How long can you hold out, Miss Clark?"

Against every woman in Denver? Hope *was* a doctor, a good one, but she was also at her wit's end...not to mention the end of her bank account.

Mrs. Chalmers moistened her lips and softened her stance a hair. "If you truly want to help people, Miss Clark, why don't you go to, oh, I don't know, India or somewhere. Some place they're desperate for medical care."

Any place Mrs. Chalmers didn't have to worry about bumping into a female doctor on the sidewalk? Well, Hope wasn't about to let this woman defeat her. But that didn't mean she had to fight the battle here in Denver where she was so outnumbered. There were other places in this big, wide world to ply her trade. Yes, some place where the people *were* desperate for medical care. India, however, seemed a touch far. "I'll consider your suggestion, Mrs. Chalmers. Thank you for coming by."

~

The intriguing aroma of human prey mingled pleasantly with the scent of dirt and cedar and the cougar lifted his head. The hope of a meal stirred grumbling in his stomach and he sniffed now with keen interest, whiskers twitching. Led by hunger, he rose from his sun-washed ledge and slipped silently between the rocks, slinking beneath the evergreen branches, staying in the shadows, tracking the peculiar but distinctive odors. Within moments he was hiding atop a boulder, peering down at two humans.

The pair—a woman and a boy—strolled carelessly through the blueberry bushes, plucking the fruit, dropping it in buckets on their arms, eating one now and again. They chattered like magpies and wandered about aimlessly, picking fruit here and there, relaxed, unhurried.

The hunger gnawing at the pit of the cat's stomach grew, but he waited.

And watched.

The boy was similar to the people who had trod these mountains for as long as cats could remember. Dark skinned, his black hair glimmered in the sun like a raven's wings.

The woman was the new breed. She was like the pale-skinned humans who had come here when the cougar had been a cub playing at his mother's feet. She did not wear animal skins or smell of sweat like the Utes and Cheyenne. She smelled of flowers and plants. Her hair was long and light, the color of grass dead from winter cold.

The cat's eyes narrowed. The young one began to wander away from her. Little by little, farther and farther. A step at a time.

The cougar considered his choices, his gaze darting from the child to the woman and back again.

Yes, the boy. Younger. Smaller. Unaware.

Tail twitching, muscles quivering, the cat slithered off the boulder and crept into the base of an evergreen thick with low-lying branches.

Naomi smiled at the sweet taste of the blueberry, pleased this patch was still producing for so late in the season. She could already smell the pie her sister Rebecca would make. One of these days, Naomi would make a serious effort to become as good a cook as her sisters. She stripped off two berries and dropped them in the basket on her arm. Two Spears, the young Indian boy with her, was not her son by blood, but Naomi loved him as if he were. Just as she loved his father, Charles. For them, she would—should—learn to cook better. She tossed a berry up into the air and caught it in her mouth. Yes, these berries would be for her own pie.

Two Spears laughed at her antics and tossed up two berries, easily catching them both in his mouth.

"Show off," Naomi said.

Grinning, the ten-year-old drifted away, his chest puffed out. He was precious and she was so glad they'd finally gotten past his resentment of being dropped on their doorstep. Well, honestly, the resentment had started before that. His mother, Hopping Bird, had been given back by Charles to her father Chief Ouray, for a remuda of horses—the trade a peaceable way to end the marriage. Charles had not known about the child. Later, Hopping Bird had fallen in love with a violent renegade by the name of One-Who-Cries, who hated Charles almost as much as he hated the entire race of white men.

Unfortunately, Charles had been forced to kill One-Who-Cries about the same time Hopping Bird had died on the White Mountain Reservation. Chief Ouray, tired of losing family to the white man, had shown up the day after Charles' and Naomi's wedding with a very special request: for Charles to raise his grandson.

She shook her head and dropped another four or five berries in the basket. Two Spears had run away it seemed about every third day, but finally, just lately, she thought he was settling in. Charles had been taking the boy out with him to check on the herd, making a real effort to—

No conscious thought shot through Naomi's mind when she saw the cougar leap off the rock. She screamed as it raced toward Two Spears, but she was moving, too. Her own body felt as if lightning had struck her, and the power of it compelled her forward at an uncanny speed. No earth beneath her feet, only electricity.

The cat lunged as Two Spears turned. A supernatural strength and fury arced through Naomi and, with a primal yell bursting from her lungs, she leaped for the boy, knocking him out of the cat's path. The claws meant for him sank into her back, burned like lava as they gouged into her flesh. She hit the ground hard, air whooshing out of her lungs. She tried to turn, but fangs clamped down on her, burrowing into the meat of her shoulder; the claws dug deep and tightened like a vice grip made of needles.

She yowled in agony. Or was it the cat?

Pain, white-hot, vicious, shot down her back, and she could feel her blood soaking her shirt. "Run, Two Spears," she yelled as she tried to fold her arms over her head and neck, to fend off teeth and claws.

Fight or die, something told her. *Oh, God, help me fight.*

Anger and terror mixed in her mind on a primitive level. The need to survive took hold. Naomi had to kill the cat. She jammed her elbow back, connecting with the heavy mass of fur on her back. The cougar shifted. His claws tightened, sunk deeper, but he let go of her shoulder.

Bellowing with rage and terror, she rolled before he could reposition his bite. She hammered the cat's snout as his claws flayed open her back and part of her side. His fangs sunk into her wrist.

Somehow a rock filled her hand and she swung it, connecting with his temple. The cat growled, angry over the hit, but only bit down harder.

"I'm not going to die, I'm not doing to die," she screamed as she hit him again and again—

An explosion rocked the air and the cat suddenly leaped skyward, twisting at a grotesque angle, and then disappeared from Naomi's sight. Unsure of where the cat had gone, she kept swinging the rock over and over, pounding the ground, and screaming, "I'm not going to die. I'm not—"

"Naomi!" Running to her, Charles holstered his gun and folded to his knees. "Naomi," he said again, breathless, as he slid his arms beneath her and lifted her off the ground.

She dropped the rock, saw the blood streaming down her arm, felt the slickness of it as Charles held her close. The fury drained away, leaving her weak, confused. She smiled at her handsome husband, those magnificent dark eyes of his and that perfectly trimmed beard. Oh, how she loved him, and it hurt her to see the fear in his face.

"I'm all right," she whispered. "Just a scratch." She suspected maybe it was a touch more, but the weariness that overcame her then stilled her concerns. She would sleep and when she woke up, everything would be fine.

Hannah lunged to her feet as Charles burst through the door of the doctor's office, a bloody and unconscious Naomi in his arms. The sight of her sister in such a state galvanized Hannah; her heart hammered so hard in her chest, she thought it might bruise her ribs.

Oh, God. "Put her on the bed," she ordered as she grabbed a tray already loaded with a few basic medical supplies. "What happened?" *Dear God, please let her be all right*, she prayed as she rushed after Charles.

"A cougar."

Hannah's stomach lurched at the word. Charles had wrapped Naomi in his own shirt and a saddle blanket, both glistening with blood. He laid her on the bed and carefully peeled back the soaked articles. Hannah stepped in close, ready for the examination, and was pleased to see his effort had stopped much of the blood, but Naomi's torso and left arm were bathed in red.

A quick survey told Hannah they weren't seeing everything. "Here, help me turn her over." Naomi's shirt and camisole hung in bloody shreds. Hannah removed the clothing and flinched at the deep, raw wounds. "Oh," she whispered softly. *Lord, this is work for a surgeon. Help me, oh, please help me.* Tears pooled in her eyes. If only she were a doctor. If only Doc Cook hadn't died. Nevertheless, Naomi was depending on her. Neither of them had a choice. "Look at the depth of those claw marks..."

Charles touched Hannah's shoulder. "We're counting on you, Hannah. You're all she's got right now." His dark eyes pleaded with her to make her whole again. "She's all I've got."

Hannah squared her shoulders, feigning a confidence she didn't feel, and nodded.

Two

CHARLES WASN'T sure his legs would carry him out of the examination room. He paused in the doorway, just to make sure. Hannah looked as terrified as he felt, blue eyes round as full moons.

God, You cannot let her die. Hannah's fished a bullet out of a man. Surely she can sew up those wounds...

She's lost so much blood, a voice whispered in a sinister tone.

He refused the dark thought with a jerk of his head. *No, Lord, you can't take her. Guide Hannah's hands.*

"Charles, would you ask Emilio to send Mollie down?"

"Is there anything I can do?" he asked, surprised by the break in his voice.

"No. Mollie knows how to ready certain things I'll need."

"He's outside with Two Spears. I'll send him on to find her."

Outside, Charles was only a little surprised to find Two Spears sniffling on the front porch, the young man Emilio patting his back. Emilio had been with Charles now for some time. Initially doing grunt work around the Iron Horse, while his sister Rose entertained customers, the teenager had wound up becoming an integral part of the McIntyre family. Hispanic, only about eighteen or so, he too, wore his hair long and straight, like Two Spears. And he'd proven himself to be honest and reliable. A good *man* in the making.

"Emilio, Hannah needs Mollie on the double."

"Sí." The young man leaped to his feet. "I'll find her." He hurried to his horse, swung up in the saddle and raced off toward Defiance's main street, only one row of buildings over. Charles waited for the sound of the horse's feet to fade before he dropped down beside Two Spears. He wished for his hat, but for the life of him couldn't recall where he'd left it. A sign of his rattled state of mind. He glanced at Two Spears and considered how much worse his nerves must be.

"She'll be all right," he said, attempting to use his most gentle Southern drawl to shore up the statement with confidence and peace—things which he did not feel at the moment. She was torn and bloody. His stomach clenched at the images. "And I'm glad you're not hurt."

The boy dropped his head to his knees and shook his head. "The cougar should have jumped me. He was coming for me."

Charles dropped his hand on the boy's back. "Naomi...?" He faded off, already knowing what happened.

"She saw him and jumped between us."

Charles shook his head. Exactly what he would have expected his lovely, fearless bride to do. She could have done no less. Probably didn't even think about it.

"She told me to run. At first, I...I..." Two Spears shook his head. "I did nothing, but she was screaming and...and then I picked up a big rock..."

"And I saw you throw it, Two Spears. You did what you could."

"No, no." He sat up straighter, his little brown face

contorted with shame, chin quivering. "I am no warrior. I am a coward."

"No, you are not a coward," Charles said firmly. "Don't ever think that of yourself. You tried to help her."

"I will kill that cat and bring back his hide."

"You stay away from up there." Concerned, Charles laid a hand on the boy's neck and gave him a reassuring pat. "I hit him. He's dead already." He'd rushed his shot, but had had no choice at the time. "The buzzards have already picked him clean, so you forget about that cat and stay off the ridge."

The boy offered only silence. Charles firmly clutched his shoulders, turning the child to him. "Give me your good word you won't go after the cat."

Fury twisted Two Spears' features. Scowling, his sable eyes burning, he finally gave his father a short, sharp nod.

～

Naomi came awake slowly. Before she opened her eyes, she took in the scent of freshly laundered sheets, the smell of alcohol, and a sharp ache throbbing in her back and shoulder.

Upon further consideration, she decided her left arm didn't feel normal, either. She shifted and realized she was lying on her stomach in the bed. Not her and Charles' bed, though. This mattress was hard and lumpy.

She thought to roll over on to her back, but the attempted motion brought an eruption of more pain from her side and shoulder, and she groaned. Rolling back onto her face, the cougar's scream echoed in her head and she remembered.

Blood-chilling screams, claws, pain...and Charles. She breathed a little easier.

"Was that you, Naomi?"

Hannah's voice. Naomi nodded, tried to speak, but only a hoarse whisper escaped her.

"Here, just a moment." Hannah came alongside the bed, lowered herself to eye level. "You can't lie on your back yet, but you can try to sit up."

Naomi nodded, and Hannah helped her. After much groaning, painful tightness in too many places, she managed to swing her feet over the edge and straighten up. Hannah had a glass of water waiting. The first sip tasted wonderful and awoke a deep thirst. Naomi tried to guzzle it, but Hannah wrestled it away.

"Drink it slowly."

Naomi wanted to argue, but Hannah clearly wasn't going to hand the glass back until Naomi agreed. She nodded and the water returned to her hand. She finished the water in four sips and licked her lips. "Is Two Spears all right?" she asked, pleased her voice was working, though it was a bit raspy.

"Fine."

"What happened to me? Was it the cat?"

"Yes."

"How bad?" When Hannah didn't answer right away, Naomi pinned her with an expectant stare.

"You've got a total of thirty-five stitches."

"Thirty-fi...?" Naomi trailed off. She didn't even want to say the number. "Am I...all right?" She touched her face, worried the cat had done some ugly damage there. She felt something on her cheekbone.

"Only three stitches in your face." Hannah smiled weakly. "I tried to make them tiny."

"Thank you. What aren't you telling me?"

Her sister took a deep, resigned breath. "I don't know that your shoulder will be all right. And you're going to have some pretty good scars."

Naomi let that sink in. Scars weren't ideal. She didn't want Charles to have to look at her mangled body, but maybe, in time, the damage would fade and not be very noticeable.

Hannah poured Naomi another glass of water and then sat down beside her on the bed. "I did the best I could, Naomi. I'm sorry. I'm not even a real nurse."

Naomi didn't sip, thirsty as she was. She lowered the glass to her lap. "I know you did the best you could. I'll never fault you—"

Hannah burst into sobs and buried her face in her hands. Naomi gingerly lifted her good arm, finding any movement hurt, and rested it across Hannah's back. "Hannah, Hannah. Please don't do this to yourself. I'm alive and I'm fine. Stitches heal. Scars fade. The cougar could have killed me."

Her sister shook her head back and forth several times, fighting for control. Finally, she managed to get her voice back. "You don't understand. You lost the baby."

Three

CHARLES SAT down in the chair next to Naomi's bed and took her hand, delighted she was awake. The stitches in her cheek and arms, the enormous bandage on her shoulder, the dozens of bloody scratches—they made his stomach roll. She could have died. Yet, she radiated love for him. Green eyes that glittered like an emerald, long, golden hair cascading down around her shoulders. Her little pug nose that he could tweak if not for her injuries. He had become a complete and unutterable fool for love. The woman had ruined him in the best way possible.

"You're awake. How do you feel?"

"Right as rain."

What Naomi could *not* do was lie to him. Never had been able to. Her little tale-tale signs of a tense brow, a mist of sweat on her upper lip, the unusually stiff set to her mouth warned him something was amiss, beyond her injuries.

He squeezed her hand, a wiggle of concern returning. "What's wrong?"

She looked away. "Isn't this enough?"

"You know you can't lie to me, princess. There's something else. I can see it on your face."

"I'm just sore."

"Naomi." He turned her face to him and he searched it, looking for answers, his concern blossoming into trepidation. What could she be hiding? "Tell me what's wrong." Tears pooled in her eyes and her chin quivered. There were few things that frightened Naomi, most especially to the point of tears. Really concerned now, he said firmly, "Tell me."

His gentle command seemed to strengthen her and she nodded. "I'm sorry, Charles. I didn't know. If I had, I would have been more careful. I would have been using the buggy or —" Her voice broke and she stopped.

"Naomi, whatever you're trying not to tell me, I'm sure it's not nearly as bad as you think."

She hid her face in her hands, took a deep breath and said, "I lost the baby, Charles."

"What ba—" He bit off the question as clarity dawned. *Dear God, we had a child?* Everything in him sagged as he tried to absorb the news, its implications. His and Naomi's—

His thoughts hurtled back to an evening, one night last year, when she'd confessed she wasn't sure if she could have children. Would he still love her, want her? One of the few fears he knew she harbored. Of course, he'd told her he loved her no matter what, and he'd meant it.

Which enabled him to see the light in this heartbreak, and not just the darkness. He tugged on his red, silk vest and straightened up. "Naomi..." Moved by her pain and her fear, he slid onto one knee in front of her and clutched her hands, pulling them from her face. "I'm sorry. For us both. But we will be all right." He tucked a stray strand of gold behind her ear, wondering if he should say something cavalier like, 'we can keep trying.' He decided to say as little as possible until he had a better handle on his emotions.

She offered him a tremulous smile. "You're so understanding. It's hard for me, though. I want to give you a child. I don't want to fail you as a wife."

"Oh, good Lord, woman. Don't speak nonsense. I told you once before the West is a hard place to live. Bad things happen. We move on. Relying on grit and perseverance."

"You said those were my strengths."

He took that to mean he could at least broach the question. "Perseverance. Can we keep trying or...?" *Or?* "Will it endanger your health? I would not lose you, Naomi. Not even for a child—"

She raised her hand to stop him. "Hannah thinks the attack was simply too much for my body. She sees no reason we can't keep trying. As far as she can tell, everything seems normal."

Charles pulled back, drifting his hand down Naomi's injured shoulder and arm. The potential *personal* danger of not having a doctor in Defiance had not hit him with any tangible impact until Naomi had spoken those words: *as far as she can tell.*

"Hannah is no doctor. She is not even a schooled nurse."

What if Naomi had some condition that would put her life at risk with every pregnancy? Hannah could sew up wounds, remove bullets, treat fevers. But she was no doc—

"This just wasn't the right time, Charles. We have to try to accept it and move on." She shrugged. "So I keep telling myself."

What if next time the pregnancy claimed the baby *and* Naomi, Charles wondered. Horrified at the thought, he surged to his feet and strode to the window to look out, at the town, at anything but his wife—the most precious gift in his life. Ever. And he'd failed her.

"Charles, what's the matter?"

Anger rose up in him. This situation simply wouldn't do. He wanted to kick himself for having not addressed it sooner. He'd been too busy wallowing in grief and guilt over the mine explosion. So many men dead and buried beneath their feet. He'd tried to hide from the remorse with a stream of cattle and lumber deals, with projects for building up the town. He'd blinded himself to this potential for a medical disaster. Adding insult to injury, Naomi had been out in those woods with his son. Mothering his mistake.

Disgusted, he swiped a hand over his mustache and sighed. "I'm sorry, Naomi, but I will make this right. I will find you the finest doctor money can buy." He turned back to her, shaking his head. "*I* failed *you*. Defiance should never have been without a doctor."

"You didn't fail me." She shifted, flinched with the movement, tried to sit up straighter. "Anyone in this town could have attempted to find a replacement for Doc. The responsibility didn't fall solely on you."

He begged to differ. Having built this town, run it, literally killed for it, he had claimed Defiance as his kingdom years ago. Monarchs had responsibilities, his personal faith in God not withstanding. *Lord, keep her healthy and I will find us a doctor.*

"No, it falls squarely on my shoulders, Naomi, and I will rectify the deficiency immediately."

Four

CHARLES SAT AT HIS DESK, tapping a ledger with a pencil, not seeing a thing in front of him. He had drafted an ad for a doctor and wired it to several larger newspapers. A high salary, free living accommodations, an open tab at the hotel's restaurant. A hardscrabble mining town wasn't any medical professional's first choice, no matter the compensation, but Charles had faith the right man would answer the ad.

Brannagh, the brawny, fifty-something Irishman who had gone from working as Charles' bartender to more of a personal assistant, knocked on his half-open door but didn't come in. "The men from the railroad."

"Ah. Yes." He dropped the pencil and came back to the matters at hand. "Thank you. Show them in."

A moment later Brannagh held the door for two rotund, heavily whiskered men in black suits, both cradling their hats. Charles rose to greet them and they shook hands across his desk. "Bob, Henry. Good to see you." Exchanging pleasantries, the men settled in the waiting chairs. "Can I get you anything. Coffee, a drink?"

Both men declined and he nodded for Brannagh to depart. When the door shut, he sat and Bob dove in. "Let's get to it, McIntyre. We don't want you to build your own spur line. Let us buy into it and share some of the other risks."

Charles leaned back and plucked a cheroot from his pocket, and a match from a box on his desk. Lighting the smoke, he said, "And some of the reward as well."

"Naturally. That's only good business."

"But I told you in my letter, I have no interest in reopening the mine."

"Then sell it," Henry said. "Let a mining conglomerate run it. The mine needs to be open to truly make the spur line a viable investment."

"I don't need your money to build the line."

The two men exchanged irritated glances. "We're businessmen, McIntyre. A spur line and a mine make Defiance an excellent investment and we want in. We can provide the capital to transform the town into a real prize. Jobs bring in men. Schools and churches and dress shops will bring in families. Defiance will blossom. Lumber and ranching alone won't do it."

"It has barely been a month. Twelve men died in that explosion, Bob. There's still too much healing that needs to be done." In the town, and in his own heart. McIntyre, taking a puff of the cigar, watched the smoke curl in front of him and tried to imagine watching men go back down into that pit. He certainly would never send them. Ever.

"You need to think this over," Henry said, leaning forward. "What Defiance needs to heal is prosperity. Families coming in and putting down roots. We want to help you build a vibrant, healthy community. With a doctor."

Charles didn't try to hide his surprise.

"We saw the ad in the Denver Post."

He did want all that for Defiance, especially the physician.

But the mine...it hung around his neck like an albatross. "And I welcome your help," he said, warring with his uncertainties, "but I won't be opening the mine." He had to suffer for a while first. His penance. Bob and Henry couldn't understand that, however.

"We've made a good, solid offer to you for the future of Defiance, for your railroad. You should think about it before closing the door."

"I am not closing the door, but I am not reopening the mine."

"Then you will sell it?" Bob said with too much confidence.

"Perhaps. Eventually." He crushed out the cheroot. "When we've healed."

"You Southerners," Henry spat. "You're too emotional."

"You Yankees are too detached. People matter."

Bob scratched his muttonchops, lifting a quizzical brow at Charles. "You've changed, McIntyre. I don't think I like it."

Charles chuckled. "Well, your opinion of me will most certainly disturb my sleep tonight."

Matthew Miller tore the fine into little pieces, placed them in the palm of his hand and blew them right back into the face of Sheriff Pender Beckwith. Piercing hazel eyes, a gaunt face like a skeleton, the tough-as-rawhide peace officer could stare a hole through most men and follow it up with a bullet.

As the pieces of paper drifted to the saloon floor, the man's edgy expression darkened to something that almost scared Matthew...almost. "Miller, I could consider that assaulting an officer."

Matthew was a big man with a wide chest and arms the size of oaks. He liked using his size to intimidate people but he knew

Beckwith wasn't cowed by such. Miffed, he leaned against his mahogany bar. "Sheriff, I'm a busy man and I'm sick of these fines." He grabbed a bottle and slid it between him and the lawman. "Why don't you have a drink—on the house—and we'll let this slide."

"And I could consider that a bribe."

Matthew clenched his teeth, pondered the man a moment, then raised is hands in surrender. "Fine. I'll go by the Iron Hor —er, I mean, the *town hall* in the morning and pay this one, too." He could barely call the old saloon that without sneering.

Beckwith rested his hand on the butt of his .44. Not a threat, Matthew knew, just a lawman's way. "I'm sick of wasting my time serving you with fines for running prostitutes. I'm gonna push for arresting the girls and confiscating your tents."

"You wouldn't throw a gal in jail who's just trying to make a living. You that cold-hearted?"

"It'd be doing 'em a favor. The living conditions are better in my jail."

"You try to confiscate anything and I'll sic my attorney on this town."

Beckwith's eyes narrowed. "You'd best send him a telegram then. Have him at the ready." The old lawman glanced at the pieces of paper on the floor, dusted one off his shoulder with disdain, turned, and marched out of the Crystal Chandelier.

The nearly *empty* Crystal Chandelier.

Only two customers watched the sheriff's exit with bland curiosity. Mathew flexed and clenched his fingers over and over for the next few minutes while he tried to cool down. Pondering Beckwith's threat, he acknowledged he couldn't keep doing business this way. He not only had to do something to get some warm bodies visiting the girls, he needed to get some warm bodies into the Crystal Chandelier. His lumber mill wasn't making enough money to keep all this afloat.

He cursed Delilah one more time for dumping this mess in his lap. He'd come to Defiance expecting to find a wide-open, rip-roarin', Godless den of debauchery. Instead, a mine explosion and the deaths of twelve men had sucked the life out of the town, and, apparently, the infamous madam. She'd dropped the keys to the place in his hand and climbed aboard a stage headed who knew where.

She had, at least, left behind Otis. The former slave from Haiti—practically the size of an island—the black man was working over in the corner, staining chairs. He was helpful, quiet, obedient, and a lot of muscle should the need arise. He had told Matthew he did not wish to leave the position which he'd held for Delilah. He was a sort of jack-of-all-trades, good and bad. Matthew had suspected—still did, in fact—that the mountain of a man would be well worth his meager pay.

Two well-dressed—and clearly well-fed—businessmen sauntered in, pulling his thoughts back to the room. They broke off their conversation as they surveyed the quiet saloon. A familiar sense of desperation clawed at Matthew. "Gentlemen," he called, moving behind his bar. "What can I get you?"

The two men exchanged puzzled glances, but one shrugged as they approached the bar. "Business looks a little slow," he said, scratching an impressive beard. "Lumber and ranching not bringing in the customers?"

"Just a little slow at the moment." Annoyed at the observation, Matthew poured two whiskeys. "On the house." He slid the shots over to them. "I'm Matthew Miller, the owner. I also own the lumberyard."

"I'm Bob Tillman."

"Henry Hathaway."

"Gentlemen, good to meet you."

Bob, the one with the impressive muttonchops, again surveyed the saloon. "McIntyre says the lumber and cattle operations should make up for the loss of the mine, but we disagree. What say you, sir?"

Matthew tilted his head, curious who these two were. Henry's gold tie pin with *Union Pacific* stamped on it answered the question. "You're with the railroad?"

"Yes. And we'd like to invest in McIntyre's spur line down to Gunnison, but it's just not viable without the mine. Would you beg to differ?"

"I hear he's gonna build that spur line with you or without you."

"We'd prefer with. We see innumerable opportunities for more investment in Defiance—if the mine is running. He doesn't agree."

"Sounds like you want a piece of it all." The two men did not voice any disagreement. Ideas dancing in his brain, Matthew picked up a towel and began wiping down his bar. "A couple hundred miners are a small town all on their own. More so than just a big handful of cowboys and lumberjacks."

Bob nodded. "Our point exactly."

"But McIntyre sees lumber and ranching expanding." Which would be fine, if Matthew could hold out.

"Or open the mine," Henry said, teasing in his voice, "and have a town full of miners practically overnight. A much faster payout."

What Matthew would call a lifeline. "He's hell-bent on not reopening."

"We got that sense, yes. However, the ad for a physician in Defiance with very generous compensation leads us to believe he has a weakness. The town. He wants to see it grow and be taken care of. The mine would spur more growth. A doctor would assure quality care for the citizens."

The weakness wasn't the town as much as it was Naomi and

her recent tangle with the cat. These yahoos didn't necessarily need that information, though, Matthew thought.

"We believe he will come around to selling," Bob said. "If the right investors with a generous package of their own show up." Bob and Henry exchanged glances again, this time knowing ones.

"You two gonna round up those generous investors?"

"I think we're going to try. You want in?"

Matthew could tell the question was asked in jest. After all, a saloon-owner wasn't loaded with enough money to buy into a million-dollar mine. Once upon a time, before sinking nearly everything he had into this place and the lumberyard, he had been. "Ah, maybe someday. Once this place starts paying off."

The gentlemen chuckled and motioned to the bottle for another shot. As he poured, though, Matthew decided maybe buying into the mine was something he should consider. Just not with these two chee chuckers.

Billy Page let himself into Doc Cook's office, fully expecting to see his betrothed Hannah tending to a patient or at the very least organizing medical supplies. To his consternation, the office was empty and quiet as Christ's tomb.

"Hannah?" He listened but heard nothing. Assuming he'd missed her somewhere between the mercantile and the hotel, he turned to go, but then did catch a slight tap or thump in the back of the building. Maybe she went to the privy. He waited another moment, but still she did not appear.

Curious, a touch concerned, he let himself out the back door. He breathed a little sigh of relief when he found her sitting on the back stoop, face turned to the sky, the late afternoon rays of the September sun gleaming off her long, golden braid. Fall was nearly upon them. It was tempting to enjoy the fading warmth while they could.

"May I join you?"

She didn't open her eyes, but nodded and smiled. "Of course."

He dropped beside her and copied her pose. "Feels good. But a touch drier than it has been."

"It'll change. Ian said rain is coming. His joints are bothering him."

Billy nodded. Her brother-in-law's arthritis was a fairly accurate weather predictor.

They sat in comfortable silence for a spell, but he'd come determined to ask her something. "Hannah, ever since Naomi got jumped by the cougar, you've been different."

"Different how?"

He shrugged a shoulder. "A little distracted, or sad. I'm not sure. And, of course, being a man, I have to assume I might be the problem." He hoped the jest might work a smile from her.

He heard one in her voice when she answered, "No, it's not you."

"Then what?"

She took a moment to respond. "Naomi is going to be pretty scarred up from the cat."

"That's not your fault. I saw the stitches you did. Best you could have done."

She huffed in what sounded like frustration. "It's not just that. Naomi...Naomi had a miscarriage."

Billy opened his eyes and looked at her. "Surely you don't think you could have done anything to prevent it?"

She huffed again then met his gaze. "I just wish I knew more. Could have done more. I don't know...I—I know just enough to know how much I *don't* know. It's frustrating."

Billy rested his elbows on his knees and tapped his fingertips together, wondering what she was getting at. "Do you want to call off the wedding? Go to nursing school?"

What was another delay? The circuit preacher had been rerouted weeks back due to a flood that had caused several deaths over in Animas Forks. A four-week window had expanded to eight. He was once more scheduled to come to Defiance in a month. Short of another disaster. Was it a sign?

His meandering thoughts gave Hannah long minutes to respond. Finally, she said, "Sometimes I don't know what I want, but I do know I don't want to call off the wedding."

"I don't want you giving up anything to marry me."

"I don't think I am."

"I want you to be happy, Hannah. If you're serious about nursing school, we could move back East together. I've got the money to open a business there. Go to nursing school and we'll hire a nanny for Little Billy."

Her brow twitched at the suggestion. "A nanny? I don't know...but you'd do that for me?"

He reached out and took her braid lightly in his hand. The play of sunlight in her blonde locks never ceased to amaze him. Or how her stunning eyes could change from lighthearted, cornflower blue to somber sapphire, depending on her mood. Now they were leaning toward sapphire.

"I'd do anything for you. You and little Billy are my life." He'd not meant to sound so serious, but the truth carried its own weight.

She touched his hand and smiled tenderly. "I love you, Billy Page. Now, you squirmed out of marrying me once. In four weeks, a preacher is tying the knot."

She kissed him, but her lips didn't distract him from the meat of their conversation. She'd pretty much ignored his suggestion about all of them moving for nursing school.

Which, to him, meant she was thinking about it.

~

Icy rain drops spit and spattered across Emilio's and Bones' path. The little sorrel shook, casting off the thin layer of water that was trying to blanket him. Emilio followed the horse's lead and shook off his coat and brushed off his legs. Which were getting cold. Good thing town wasn't much further. Thinking about Mollie warmed him right up, though.

It had taken some time for his affections to move away from Hannah, but the more time he spent with Mollie, the more their rough backgrounds had created a bond. A former Flower, she'd done some things just to survive. Orphaned at five and raised by a wolverine for a sister, Emilio had done no better. He and Mollie knew each other's sordid past and it had removed all the pretense between them. He was comfortable with her in a way he'd never been with anyone else.

And because he believed that, she scared him.

Suddenly aggravated by the cold drops biting him in the face, he steered Bones off the road and took a shortcut through a forest of white-trunked Aspens. The golden leaves offered some protection and he patted his horse. "Better, boy, sí?"

He removed the Stetson and shook his black hair. Maybe he should cut it. None of the other ranch hands wore their hair this long. Emilio's was long enough to make a short ponytail.

Without the black cowboy hat, he looked every bit the Mexican he was. None of the men said that to his face, of course. He was the second-in-command at the ranch, under Lane, but folks whispered about how partial Mr. McIntyre was to him. They couldn't know the things Mr. McIntyre and Emilio had been through. Fights, Indian attacks, explosions, to name a few.

They had forged a friendship that Emilio valued. He almost

considered the man to be like a father. Closest thing he'd ever had, anyway. And he had suggested pursuing Mollie.

Emilio straightened up in the saddle and replaced the hat, cutting free with a big smile. Mr. McIntyre had never given him bad advice.

A half-hour later, Emilio and Bones merged onto a jostling, muddy Main Street and made their way to the Trinity Inn for dinner. Mollie would wait on him, finish her shift, and then the two of them had planned a walk down by the river, weather permitting. He enjoyed her company and one reason he was so comfortable with her: he could just be himself.

Buoyed by the anticipation of the meal and the company, he tied up in front of the inn and slipped inside. The dining room was still packed, but his little table over by the kitchen door was waiting on him.

He nodded to a few of the boys from the ranch who had come into town as well, and claimed his seat. A minute later a delicate, fair hand set a glass of water in front of him and he looked up into her beautiful, welcoming face.

Mollie's blue eyes glowed with warmth and tenderness. "Good evening, sir."

He grinned at her formal tone. "Good evening, señorita. What is on the menu tonight?"

"Elk steaks. Mashed potatoes. Peas. Beets. Apple pie for dessert." Emilio's stomach grumbled. They ate well at the ranch, just not that well. Mollie laughed richly, hugging the tray in her arms. "You poor thing. I'll rush your meal so you don't fall out right here in the restaurant."

"Would you still like to go for a walk this evening, when your shift is done?"

Some color rushed to Mollie's cheeks. A tantalizing smile teased her lips. "I would love to."

She started to walk away and Emilio surprised himself by taking her hand, halting her retreat. "It-it is good to see you, Mollie. I miss you when I'm at the ranch."

She squeezed his hand and said flirtatiously, "Then you'll just have to come in more than once a week."

Five

HOPE COULD HAVE BEEN indignant about her plan, the subterfuge being wholly beneath her. Yet, if she wanted to serve as a doctor, well, lying about her credentials might be necessary. At least at first. Until she saw some patients and gained the trust of the community. Then her fair gender wouldn't be an issue. She had to believe that.

For the hundredth time, as weak, gray light flashed through the pines and into the stuffy stagecoach, she took the newspaper from her medical case. Folded open to the advertisement, she read again the request for a doctor in Defiance. A fine salary, living accommodations, array of patients. She was taking a huge chance coming to Defiance rather than writing, but she believed she could convince this Charles McIntyre Hope Clark was the answer to his ad.

When the stage stopped, she asked that her trunk be sent to the hotel and for directions. The driver, jumping down from his seat, pointed west and said, "The Trinity Inn is open now and they have a fine restaurant, too."

At the mention of food, Hope's stomach grumbled and she

touched the reticule hanging from her wrist. Yes, a bite to eat and then she'd search out Mr. McIntyre. She thanked the driver and headed down the busy street. Tugging her coat closer against a weak smattering of rain, she took the time to assess the town.

She'd heard that Defiance was a clamoring mecca of mining opportunities. It didn't strike her as such today. Yes, there were miners with heavily laden mules moving up and down the muddy street, but also cowboys riding through town, and lumberjacks loading supplies into wagons at the mercantile. There was also plenty of elbow room between them all. On her way out west, Hope's trip had taken her to Deadwood and the pace in that mining town had been downright frenetic.

Not so here. Defiance was bustling, but at a measured pace. The reported Gold Fever, if she didn't miss her guess, had broken. The patient's temperature had returned to something akin to normal. She didn't know yet if she should be disappointed or grateful.

Up ahead she saw a sign for The Trinity Inn sitting high on a new, golden-hued, two story building. White rocking chairs lined both the front porch and the balcony above. She hoped the weather would clear as she could see herself resting her weary bones in one of those chairs and watching the sunset.

Hope found a break in the traffic and scurried across the street to the hotel. Once inside, the scent of fresh pine and steaks struck her instantly. The hotel was new, indeed, as evidenced by the bright rugs and polished floor and the bright velveteen of the lobby furniture.

Off to her left she heard the clink of silverware and rumbling chatter and double-doors opened to the dining room. Directly in front of her, a wide staircase led to the second floor. Two well-dressed, middle-aged women descending them gave Hope a blandly curious glance and continued on into the restaurant. She nodded politely and crossed the lobby to the desk.

A pudgy young girl, maybe twenty, with a round, cherubic face greeted her. "Good evening. Welcome to the Trinity Inn. Will you be needing a room or are you here to dine?"

"Yes, a room. I'll need it for at least two days. Hopefully that'll be all it takes," she muttered underneath her breath.

The girl spun the register to her. "Just passing through then?" she asked, handing Hope a fountain pen.

"No, actually I'm hoping to meet with Mr. Charles McIntyre regarding a position—" She stopped to admire the writing instrument, an unusual item in a rustic town. She hadn't seen any outside of New York City.

The clerk chuckled. "It's called a fountain pen. The ink is in the chamber."

"Yes, I am familiar with them. I just didn't expect to see one in Defiance. They're quite the talk in the East."

"We've got lots of surprises here. There's a saying in mining towns: with money, men, and mules, you can get anything you want." She pointed over her shoulder. "Our new kitchen stove come direct fr—"

"Señora Betsy," a terrified voice called from the dining room. "Get Miss Hannah." A Hispanic woman skidded to a stop in the doorway to the dining room, waving her arms frenetically. "A man is choking. I do not know what to do."

Still holding the pen in one hand and her medical bag in the other, Hope rushed to the woman. "Show me."

The commanding tone in her voice spurred the woman to react. Without questioning, she turned and raced back into the dining room. A crowd of people half-surrounded a man on the floor. Another waitress held his head as he thrashed about with fading strength, his face turning bluer by the second. His motions slowed and then ceased at the same instant Hope dropped to her knees to examine him.

"He was eating a steak and then started choking," a man above her said.

She could tell immediately the patient had an extreme blockage. He would not survive till she could be ready for surgery. The pen in her hand screamed her next step.

She noted absently some motion in the crowd and she reached out, grabbing the closest hand. She thrust the pen into it as she turned to her bag. "Break that open. Make it a straw."

With practiced speed, she slid a scalpel from its velvet pocket and pulled the person with the pen to the floor. She met the wide, sapphire eyes of a girl barely more than a teenager who held up the broken pen for Hope's approval.

"Good. Now, are you squeamish?"

The girl shook her head.

"Hold his wrist and feel for his pulse. Can you do that?"

This time the young lady moved immediately to do Hope's bidding.

Hope looked up at the wide-eyed waitress still cradling the man's head. "Use your cleaning cloth to dab at the blood when I tell you to."

"Bl—blood?" the girl stammered.

Ignoring her, Hope felt along the man's throat for the cricoid cartilage, tested the flesh with her index finger and then sliced a half-inch incision to his windpipe. Immediately the blood flowed. "Your cloth, girl," she ordered impatiently. With shaking hands the waitress dabbed at the blood pouring from the wound.

Hope put the scalpel in her teeth, grabbed the broken pen from the girl checking the man's pulse, pinched the wound to open it, and inserted the instrument.

Not getting an immediate reaction, she tossed the scalpel

into her bag and pressed her lips to the broken pen. She blew into the man's lungs, paused, and then repeated the action. Again and again she blew life into him.

"Come on," she whispered, her desperation growing. He couldn't die. She'd made it to him in time. She blew more air into his lungs and the girl holding his wrist gasped. Hope looked at her.

"There's a pulse." She tilted her head, *listening* to her fingers, and nodded. "A definite pulse," she said with an air of expertise that surprised Hope. "Thready, weak, but there," the girl added as if for emphasis.

Hope nodded at the surprising impromptu nurse. "We're not done yet. I have to do surgery to remove the blockage. We need to get him to the doctor's office."

The girl picked out men in the crowd. "Bob, Wade, Emilio. Let's get him over to Doc's."

"Yes, Miss Hannah," said a tall, lean man with a badge, immediately stepping forward to help.

Six

WITH EVERY STITCH, with every order the woman barked, Hannah's estimation of her own skills as a nurse diminished like melting ice. Hannah had seen Doc perform surgeries and assisted on a few, but this stranger in Defiance was clearly a trained and very skilled nurse.

The two of them had bypassed any pleasantries and small talk and tackled the issue of the blocked windpipe forthwith. Hannah had followed orders to the best of her ability and quickly found everything requested for the surgery, standing at the ready with scalpels, needles, sutures, bandages, and alcohol.

Finally, with the procedure done and the last stitch in place, Hannah whispered across the sleeping patient to the mysterious nurse, "Why don't you go sit down for a moment and I'll get you some water."

The woman, auburn hair twisted up in the new French style, was pretty, and young, maybe in her mid-twenties. She tilted her head at Hannah, azure eyes friendly, and smiled. "You knew your way around the surgery. Around this office. You were a godsend, so to speak."

She sounded almost amazed and Hannah's sagging spirits rose again. "I helped Doc Cook out when I could. He taught me a lot. But just watching you work, I can see that there's so much more to nursing than I ever thought."

A shadow crossed the woman's face, but it passed almost instantly. She touched the patient's forehead with the back of her hand. "I don't even know your name. Mine is Do—Hope. Hope Clark."

Hannah noted the strange correction. "I'm Hannah Frink. You sound like you're from back east. Which nursing school did you go to? Have you been a nurse long? How did you wind up in Defiance?"

Hope chuckled at the onslaught of questions, but then her shoulders sagged. "I am very tired. I think I'll sit on the porch for a moment and get some cool air. Would you mind bringing me that glass of water?"

"Not at all."

Hannah delivered the drink and for the moment they sat in companionable silence, listening to the few remaining crickets sing a welcome to fall, catching notes now and again from a singer at the Crystal Chandelier and the raised voices of men, mostly laughing. A far cry from the wild-and-wooly free-for-all the town was, up until the mine had collapsed.

Charles had said at least a third of the town's population had moved on. Hannah liked the quiet, but she sensed something in it. The town seemed to be fighting for its life.

"What happened to Doctor Cook?" Hope asked and took a sip of the water. "My, it's cold. How nice."

"Doc has a springhouse out back." Hannah sighed, seeing her friend and mentor splayed out on the bed, face pale, lips blue. The glaring bruises on his face and neck. "We're not sure. He was beat up some, but we don't know if that killed him or his heart gave out."

"He was attacked?" Hope sounded alarmed at the potential for violence in the town.

"The town went through—" Hell. She almost described Delilah and her horrendous saloon and acts of retribution with that one word. "A tough time. There was a bad element here trying to take over. They caused the mine explosion. That seemed to take the wind out of them, and they left."

And a lot of folks in town still weren't happy with Beckwith for not arresting Delilah, but Hannah understood how painful a trial would have been. Maybe the sheriff had been concerned about mob violence and lynchings.

"I came here, Hannah, because I want to take up Doctor Cook's mantle. I didn't answer the ad formally. I just showed up. I want to work in a town where there is a real need."

"Well, Lord knows you're a far sight more skilled than I am —tonight proved that—but I also know Charles wants to hire a full-fledged doctor."

"No chance he'd hire a nurse now, even a very skilled one like I am?"

Hannah shrugged. "I don't know. Maybe he'd keep you on until a doctor is hired. Or even after. I don't want to speak for him." Though she suspected the man wouldn't turn away any skilled medical help.

"Hannah," Hope leaned over the arm of the rocking chair, "what kind of man is this Charles McIntyre? Is he open-minded? Does he judge people before he knows them?"

"No, he's a good man. Fair."

"How do you think he'll react to me just showing up here?"

"After what you did for Bob Ledford in there, surely he'll be glad, but there's more to this." Hannah looked out at the midnight sky, twinkling with diamonds, but saw the ugly scars marring Naomi's back, the sadness on her face when she'd told her about the baby. "Where were you two weeks ago?"

"I'm sorry?"

A chill creeping over her, Hannah rubbed her arms, rose, and went to the porch rail. The buildings up on Main Street were dark shadows, silhouetted in a weak quarter moon. "My sister Naomi was attacked by a mountain lion."

"Oh. Is she all right?"

"Yes...and no. I took care of her, did the best I could, tried extra hard with the stitches to keep them small and neat. But Naomi's wounds won't be the scars on her body. She lost the baby she was carrying, and Charles can't seem to..."

"Accept it? He thinks if there'd been a doctor here, the baby would have lived?"

"Yes. I feel so useless. Just a lowly, half-trained nurse. I can't tell him why Naomi miscarried, and I can't tell him if it will happen again, if she has some condition. So you see," she turned back to Hope, "he doesn't want a nurse. He needs a doctor. For Naomi."

"I do see."

Hope withdrew into herself for a long while and Hannah didn't bother her. Finally, the woman said softly, "Would you vouch for me when I go speak with Mr. McIntyre tomorrow? Help me to get him to let me work here...until a doctor is found?"

"Absolutely. He won't turn you away. He just may not promise you something long-term." Hannah smiled, realizing what conclusion Charles would ultimately come to and lightened her tone. "Of course, once he realizes what a blessing you would be for the doctor, you could be a circus chimpanzee and he'd keep you."

～

As always, Charles was delighted to see his sister-in-law Hannah. Her golden ponytail streaming over her shoulder, stunning blue eyes and similar pug nose reminded him of Naomi and he enjoyed the girl's company. She was as bubbly as a mountain stream and injected a room with cheer. When she knocked on his office door, however, holding her son, something in him deflated a little. Ever since Naomi had lost their baby, he'd been spending too much time thinking about a son. And, admittedly, overlooking Two Spears. *Lord, help me look past my own hurts to the boy...*

"Hannah, what a pleasant surprise." He rose and nodded at Little Billy. "And how is the young prince today?"

"Getting into everything now that he's walking." As if to prove her point, she let her son slide to the floor. Holding on to his mother's finger, the towheaded little fella ambled precariously toward Charles.

"My, look at you, young man." Charles stepped out from behind his desk and squatted to make himself an easier target for the toddler. Grinning from ear to ear, the boy let go of his mother and waddled like a drunk into Charles' arms. "Well, I'll be." He scooped up Little Billy and rose to his feet. "You'll be dancing with all the pretty gals at the parties this fall, won't you?"

"Yes, he'll be a ladies' man."

"Too handsome not to be."

Hannah giggled, shook her head. "But I know you're busy and I have to get on to the mercantile. I wanted to tell you, though, a young lady came into town yesterday."

Any statement about women coming to Defiance always made his heart stop for a moment and he set Little Billy back on the ground. "And?"

The boy toddled back to his mother. "Oh, no, it isn't bad. I think it's wonderful. She's wonderful. Bob Ledford would have died last night at the restaurant if she hadn't been there."

"Bob? What happened?"

"He nearly choked to death. Hope did a tracheotomy right there on the floor and then did the surgery on him at Doc's. She's a highly skilled nurse."

This was much better news than what it could have been and Charles breathed a sigh of relief. "You saw?"

"All of it. She came here because she knows you're looking for a doctor. She wants to stay in Defiance. Work here, assist the doctor when you hire one."

Charles returned to his seat and motioned for Hannah to claim the one in front of his desk. She shook her head and picked up her son. "I really don't have time. I just wanted to smooth the way for her. She's afraid you might turn her away, showing up without writing first and all."

"You say she's skilled?"

"The word is an understatement. I saw how fast she did that tracheotomy and I was truly impressed. I talked with her some more this morning. She graduated top of her class from Pennsylvania Women's Medical College."

"She has references, I assume."

"Yes, and she'll bring them when you meet with her."

He tapped a pencil on his ledger as his thoughts raced. "Top of her class? What of you? I know you want to nurse. What if I keep her on when the doctor is hired? What will you do?"

"I want what's best for Naomi, for Defiance. I'll help all I can and then, when you find a doctor, if there's room for me, I'll keep training. If not, I'm sure the Lord will lead me to something else."

Charles wished he could be so sure, so trusting of the Lord's will. He was working on it, of course, but it didn't seem so easy to find right now. Not when Naomi was healing from both a brutal animal attack and the loss of their child. Leaning on his own understanding seemed much easier for the moment. "It certainly couldn't hurt to have her around, then."

Hannah beamed. "Can I tell her?"

He chuckled, rose, and plucked his hat from the hook beside his desk. "I've got to get back out to the ranch. Unfortunately, it could be a month or so before I choose a doctor. So tell your nurse friend to go ahead and move into Doc's. I'll stop by in the next day or so to introduce myself and see if she needs anything."

"This afternoon," Hannah said firmly. "Naomi has an appointment this afternoon. Three o'clock."

Charles stopped. "Had my answer all figured out, did you?"

"I knew what you'd say because you want the best for Naomi. And Hope certainly has far more training than I do."

Yes, that was not a fact to be denied. "Top of her class? Well," he dropped his hat in place, "sounds as if Defiance will be fortunate to have her."

Seven

NAOMI SAT down on the front porch step, took a deep breath, and closed her eyes. The sun on her face, the buzz of a nearby bee, and the sounds of cattle mooing, cowboys shouting, and a rooster crowing off in the distance made her smile. She needed to smile. To find something to smile about.

The wounds from the cat ached and pulled uncomfortably when she moved. They seemed to make her whole body sore, but her heart hurt worse than anything. She was trying to be brave for Charles but she'd lost a baby—their child—and sometimes the grief threatened to swamp her.

In time, she told herself, *in time we'll be past this. I'll be my normal, foolishly stubborn self, right, Lord?* But she felt as if so much of the fight had gone out of her. *A baby. Our baby. A little girl? A rough and tumble boy? Oh, Lord, it's so hard to trust Your plan sometimes.*

A knot formed in her throat and she stood up with relief at the sound of the approaching wagon. It buoyed her spirits to see Charles and Two Spears riding together. He had promised he would renew his efforts to spend more time with the boy and was keeping his word.

He needs to love him like he's his only son. He may be.

She turned away from the implication and trudged stiffly out to the wagon. Charles was wearing his favorite blue suit with a gray silk vest. Two Spears was dressed in dungarees and a plaid shirt, his black, shoulder-length hair tucked behind his ears. Both of them so different, yet so similar. Every day, Naomi could see Charles more and more in the boy's face, though the child was undeniably Ute. She prayed the lineage wouldn't be a curse.

Charles handed the reins to Two Spears and climbed down for Naomi. "Your conveyance to town, your ladyship."

Smirking at his pet name, she clutched his shoulders and allowed him to lift her up to the seat. With care, she settled in, but even the gentlest movements set the stitches to talking. She winced and Charles saw it. "You're all right?"

Naomi exhaled, willing the pain away. "I will be. I just need some time."

She hadn't meant to sound so melancholy, but Charles settled beside her and dropped a reassuring arm around her waist. "Yes. Time solves everything." He looked at Two Spears. "All right, let's practice those driving skills."

The young boy practically grimaced with intense concentration as he drove the horses. He was much more comfortable in the saddle, Naomi knew, but she also had faith he'd get a handle on this new task easily.

"Now, Naomi," Charles began, "you keep in mind you are seeing a nurse today. Not a doctor. You must weigh anything she says carefully."

"I will, but a medical-school trained nurse is still quite the boon for Defiance. And I'm sure she'll be able to teach Hannah a few things. I'm excited to meet her."

The day was warm and perfect. Beneath a cloudless, blue sky Charles chatted about the herd's increased production, a couple of new hands from Texas joining the King M, and the lumber camp up on Screech Owl Ridge shooting a wolf. Mundane but comforting to hear him share his work with her. It didn't take long for her, however, to notice Two Spears' silence.

At first she had excused it as his attempt to master driving the team, but after a few miles the same grim look of determination still kept every muscle in his face frozen. She glanced at Charles and back to the boy. "Two Spears, is everything all right?" Come to think of it, he'd been unusually quiet since... her mind struggled to follow a timeline backward.

To the attack.

He shrugged an evasive answer and kept his focus on the horses. Naomi chewed on her lip. Fear in an Indian boy was probably not looked on well. But he *was* only a boy. And the attack was still delivering nightmares to her. How was it affecting him?

"You know, I'm feeling much better. These stitches will be out today and I'll be back to my old self again in no time." She decided to wade in and determine his level of fear. She leaned across Charles to speak more directly to him. "I'm ready to go and pick some more berries. I'm not afraid of the cat. In case you were wondering."

"You cannot go back," the stoic child said without looking at her. "At least not until the cat is dead."

"He is dead. It was a good shot, Two Spears," Charles reconfirmed. "He didn't get far before he dropped."

"You hit him. You did not kill him."

Both Naomi and Charles froze at the statement, made with what sounded like absolute confidence. He turned to Two

Spears. "I told you to stay away from that ridge. If you've been up there alone I'll turn you over my knee—"

"Charles," Naomi squeezed his knee and cut him off. "Two Spears, you are a courageous warrior. Charles told me you were ready to fight the cat with nothing but a rock. Just like David and Goliath. You remember that story?"

The boy seemed to relax a touch. "He killed the giant with a rock."

"Yes, he did, but you need to grow up a little more in the Lord before you go fighting lions and bears and giants, all right? Promise me you'll stay away from up there." When he didn't answer immediately, she pushed. "Give me your good word you'll stay away from the ridge. Promise me."

Grudgingly, he nodded. "I promise."

Rebecca Donoghue yawned with afternoon boredom as she stepped off the boardwalk and headed down the alley that would take her to Doc Cook's office. Only Doc Cook wasn't around anymore, and she missed the old codger. He'd been so sweet, training Hannah to be a nurse.

Rebecca emerged from the alley and scanned the quiet road left to right. Running parallel to Main Street, Parker's Path had been the main route to the Sunnyside Mine. Now...

A dust devil swirled down the empty lane in the dry fall afternoon. The few log cabins that dotted the field across from her rose above the brittle weeds like grave markers. The eerily idle Sunnyside Mine compound, the tomb for twelve men buried in the rock, sat several hundred yards up the slope.

Lord, it's just depressing back here. Will the town ever recover? Be a place to raise a family? Can it even survive without the mine?

Can our newspaper?

Rebecca pushed the nagging worries away. *One step at a time, one day at a time,* she told herself.

Doc's small office, a little, yellow clapboard box with a long front porch, sat alone and forlorn, the last visible building on the thoroughfare. Doc's house was a hundred feet up the path but hidden by a stand of pines. Movement behind a window caught Rebecca's eye and she touched the pencil at her ear to make sure it was still there. She strode with purpose up to the door, tossed her long, dark braid over her shoulder and knocked.

A curtain fluttered. Aware she was being assessed by the new occupant, Rebecca waited patiently. A moment later, a pretty young lady with auburn hair piled into a loose bun opened the door. A crisp, white apron covered her dress. Rebecca offered her hand as the woman smiled hesitantly.

Friendly, but curious caramel eyes assessed Rebecca. "Yes?"

"Hello. I'm Hannah's sister Rebecca. You're Hope, I presume?"

The two shook and Hope stepped back to let her enter. "I am. Please come in."

She'd been cleaning. The office smelled of witch hazel, turpentine, and some odors Rebecca couldn't place.

"My, if you hadn't told me you were sisters, I wouldn't have put the two of you together," the woman said, closing the door.

Rebecca fished a notepad from her pocket. "Yes, we hear that all the time. Hannah and Naomi are the petite, fair-haired beauties. I apparently was left on the doorstep by a passing Indian tribe."

Hope laughed at the old joke which Rebecca loved whipping out when she could. "I certainly don't think it was a tribe of ugly Indians," Hope assured her. "You and your sister

Hannah are beautiful. Speaking of sisters, Naomi is going to be my first patient this very afternoon."

"Hannah said she was coming to see you."

"Oh, my, Hannah has worked very hard to get things rolling here for me. I'm truly appreciative of her assistance."

"The whole town is talking about how you saved Bob. Everything Hannah has done—well, let's say you made the work of touting you easy. I don't suppose you could have had a better announcement of your arrival than saving a man's life in the middle of a crowded restaurant. I'm sure our readers are eager to learn all about you."

Hope's face tightened and her hand went to her throat. Rebecca reigned in her enthusiasm. Interviewing people had taught her to watch for tell-tale signs of discomfort.

She patted the air gently. "Please don't be nervous. You don't have to answer any questions you're not comfortable with. And I'm not looking to do an exposé. Just get enough information to help the citizens of Defiance find common ground with you. Help them feel comfortable in coming to see you."

"Yes, I nee—uh, *want* that, too."

Rebecca heard the quick correction and filed it away. "Could we sit for a moment?"

"Certainly, but I have to give you fair warning. Your sister will be here soon for a 3:30 appointment. I can't guarantee how much time we'll have to chat."

"Oh, well," Rebecca plucked the pencil from her ear, "then let's get started."

"Please, sit down." Hope motioned to the rocking chair by the stove. She grabbed a ladderback from the edge of the sitting area and dragged it closer to Rebecca, making their chat more intimate.

"Perhaps some quick basics. Your full name, where you're

from, do you have any family, are you married, will your husband be joining you if you are?"

"Hope Melinda Clark. I'm from Scranton, Pennsylvania. I have two brothers younger than myself, Josh and Caleb. Twins. My father is a doctor. I am not married. I was engaged..." She trailed off, seemed to ponder what more to say on the subject. "He was not supportive of my career choice."

Rebecca's pencil slowed. "That would be his loss. Hannah said you graduated at the top of your class."

"Yes, and I think I did that just to show him he hadn't completely broken my heart."

Rebecca nodded, appreciating the woman's spunk. "Good for you. And where did you go to school?"

"Pennsylvania Women's College of Medicine."

"And you graduated in...?"

"Oh, that was 1874."

"Four years. Where have you been employed prior to coming to Defiance?"

"I prac—I mean, nursed in my father's practice for two years before I came west. I have a bit of an adventurous spirit, as Father described my wanderlust," she added with a smirk.

"I see," Rebecca, said scribbling madly. "What's your father's name. And between there and here you worked—?"

"For a doctor in Denver." She paused, again planning her words, Rebecca assumed. "He practiced in an affluent area," Hope said slowly. "I found the patients more difficult to deal with than their ailments. I didn't feel useful there."

"And, I'm sorry, your father's name was...?"

Rebecca didn't miss the slight hesitation, but Hope answered, "Dr. James Clark."

"I see. Well, I dare say you'll have more than hangnails and bunions in Defiance."

"Yes." She smiled shyly. "It's a terrible thing to look forward to...to sickness and injury. But come they will, and I plan to do my best at caring for the citizens of Defiance."

The rattle and jangle of a buggy pulling up outside took their gazes out the window. "Oh, there's Charles and Naomi now. So, quickly, one last question, if I may."

"Of course."

"Have you delivered many babies?"

Hope smiled, as if understanding the basis of concern for the question. "Yes. At last count, fifty-one."

Rebecca closed her notebook and the two rose. "Thank you for speaking with me. I trust, if I have any follow-up questions, you won't mind if I bother you again."

Hope waved her hand. "No bother at all. Anything I can do to make the citizens of Defiance aware of me and trust me, please just ask."

～

Hope's palms went clammy as she opened the door to welcome the McIntyres. Rebecca thanked her again and then slipped out to greet her sister.

No, Hope thought, *they certainly don't look related.* Rebecca, tall, ebony hair, noble features, was at least in her early forties. Naomi was her opposite in every way and probably in her late twenties, though she moved like an eighty-year-old woman, apparently due to her recent injuries.

The man with Naomi was a real Adonis, as a friend from college would have described him. Charles McIntyre had a devilishly handsome face framed by wavy, black hair and a beard, and an athletic physique wrapped in a tailored blue suit. He moved with a confidence that Hope had seen only among men who were movers and shakers. Men who could take on the world and everything in it.

Only...

She blinked in surprise. The man repositioned his cowboy hat, took Naomi's hand, and, gazing at her as if she were the goddess Venus, assisted her down from the wagon with a firm but caring touch, intensely aware of her injuries.

He handles her as if she is more precious to him than rubies.

The snippet of the Scripture whispered in her mind, catching her off guard. She hadn't thought of the Bible, or her mother—or God for that matter—in years.

"How are you feeling today, honey?" Rebecca asked, approaching the wagon and snapping Hope back to the moment.

Mr. McIntyre eased Naomi to the ground and she gave Rebecca a pained smile. "I'm all right. Some days are better than others, but I'm all right."

"You'll start having more good days than bad, once you get those stitches out." Rebecca smirked at Mr. McIntyre. "I see you're taking good care of her."

"I am afraid of what Hannah might do to me if I don't," he answered in a thick Southern drawl that, Hope thought, gave his words an almost hypnotic lilt.

They all laughed and Rebecca switched to the passenger still in the wagon. A boy of about ten with dark skin, long straight hair, fiercely dark eyes. An Indian, though dressed in western clothing. "Two Spears," Rebecca said, "would you like to walk to the mercantile with me while Naomi sees the nurse? They're all stocked up on licorice and I have a nickel with your name on it."

The boy gazed at the McIntyres with unveiled, unabashed pleading in his expression. Naomi and Mr. McIntyre nodded, laughing, and he jumped to the ground. Rebecca turned back to Hope and waved. "Thank you again, Hope."

"My pleasure."

"You can come get Two Spears at the town hall," she said to her sister as she and the boy walked away.

The couple gave their approval and then headed for Hope and her front porch. "Mr. McIntyre. Mrs. McIntyre. It's my pleasure to meet you. I'm Hope Clark."

They shook hands and she ushered them inside, Mr. McIntyre removing his cowboy hat as they entered. Walking to the center of the room, where an examination table sat surrounded by cabinets, shelves of supplies, and counters for working space, Hope turned. "I don't mean to be presumptuous, but I found the lack of privacy for this particular area unsettling. I've strung a curtain to separate it from the waiting area."

Both Naomi and Mr. McIntyre seemed to regard her with surprised admiration, each lifting an eyebrow at her statement. They surveyed the wire dissecting the main room, a curtain hanging on it but bunched tightly against the wall.

"I think that's a wonderful idea," Naomi said. "I don't know why Doc Cook never did it."

"Because it will make the waiting area the size of a broom closet," Mr. McIntyre said resting his hat on the hook by the door, making Hope wonder if she'd made a mistake.

"Men," she said, hoping to sound jovial, "tend to overlook such simple things but simple things can provide so much comfort to a patient. And I do wish to put the patient first."

"As you should," Naomi said, giving Mr. McIntyre a sideways glance.

"Yes, well," he said, tucking a thumb into the gun belt at his waist, "Doc was a good man and a good doctor, but he was also pretty cut-and-dried. To the point. No frills."

"I don't mind a few frills," Hope said, smiling at Naomi who beamed back at her and her spirits soared. If she could win this *precious jewel* over, Mr. McIntyre was sure to follow. "So, Mrs. McIntyre, if you'd like to step into examination room one," Hope stepped back and motioned toward the little room, "I can answer any questions you might have, Mr. McIntyre, about my credentials while she undresses. My references are on the window ledge there behind you."

As he moved toward the window, Hope slipped into the room with Naomi. "Hannah said you were attacked by a mountain lion and she put thirty-five stitches in your shoulders and side?"

"Yes. And a few other places."

"I can't imagine how terrifying that must have been."

Naomi started undoing the buttons on her blouse. "I kept praying for the strength to fight."

"Fight?" Hope repeated as she helped the woman slip out of her shirt. "It has been my experience most people in a similar situation pray for help."

"Naomi, you'll discover," Mr. McIntyre said through the door, "is not a woman to run from a fight, even when she should."

Hope half-smiled at Naomi. "We might have something in common."

"Lovely," Mr. McIntyre dead-panned.

Both women giggled and Hope's confidence grew. "Well, let's start by taking a look at your stitches."

Hope was quite impressed with Hannah's work and said so aloud as her gaze drifted intently over the wounds. Neat, precise sutures followed the tracks of claw marks down Naomi's shoulder and side. Some of the stitches on smaller wounds had been removed and they looked as if Hannah had done a skillful job there as well. Naomi was healing in fine order.

"Miss Clark," Mr. McIntyre called, "these references are from your father and a few of his patients. Where have you been since," he paused, "since '77?"

"A doctor in Denver. As I told Hannah, I did not care for

his wealthy patients. They were tedious to deal with." Hope lifted off a bandage at the top of Naomi's shoulder and examined several unstitched puncture wounds—bite marks. A raging pink, they were deep but clean. Still, the cat had done a lot of damage. "Can you raise your left arm for me?"

"He would not give you a reference?" Mr. McIntyre asked.

"Frankly, Mr. McIntyre, I didn't leave Denver on the best terms." Not a lie exactly. Naomi raised her arm and Hope saw her flinch when the elbow was about shoulder level. "I'm sorry, that's painful for you?"

Naomi hesitated an instant, then nodded. "The bite hurts. Down deep."

Trying to mask her concerns for her patient's injury and Mr. McIntyre's curiosity, Hope kept her face blank as she pressed lightly on Naomi's deltoid and trapezius. Naomi winced and tensed her muscles.

"I'm sorry. I know this is uncomfortable," Hope apologized. Outside, Mr. McIntyre grunted and Hope tried to offer a truthful explanation. "My bedside manner when it comes to foolish complaints"—She had Mrs. Chalmers squarely in mind as she spoke—"Well, perhaps I could learn to be a bit more diplomatic."

"Perhaps," he said flatly.

Hope turned her full attention to Naomi, resolving to deal with Mr. McIntyre later. "The cat may have torn a tendon." She couldn't know for sure and only time would tell. "Such injuries are difficult to heal, so use your arm as little as possible over the next two weeks and then I'll examine you again. Is the pain manageable, or do you feel you need laudanum?"

"No."

Hope nodded, encouraged by the woman's grit. "All right. Now, we'll get the rest of these stitches out today, and then," Hope paused, sensitive to the situation. "Hannah said you lost the baby you were carrying. And that you didn't know you were pregnant. Is that correct?"

"I had missed a monthly. Was late on the next one. I was beginning to suspect when...when the cat attacked." Naomi turned pleading green eyes to Hope. "Hannah said the loss of the blood could have caused the miscarriage and that I might not have anything to worry about. As far as getting pregnant again."

The shuffling of papers and pacing footsteps on the other side of the door stopped. Hope nodded. "Entirely possible. Blood loss, shock. Early in a pregnancy is the most dangerous time for a fetus. But we'll get to all that. Let's take out these stitches first."

A little while later, Hope performed Naomi's ladies' exam and made an unexpected discovery. She paused her movements and Naomi seemed to sense something.

"Is anything wrong?"

Hope removed the speculum and stood up. "You can get dressed now. Let me wash up and I'll join you and Mr. McIntyre shortly."

Eight

NAOMI DRESSED and joined Charles in the sitting area. He rose, pulled her into an embrace, and she melted against him, enjoying the scents of lilac soap and apple-tinged tobacco. "That didn't take very long. Stitches all out?"

She nodded, breathing him in—scents so uniquely, wonderfully him.

"How do you feel?"

At the moment? "Peaceful." She snuggled into him and he kissed the top of her head. "I'm stiff," she said, recognizing the seriousness of his question. "And it's going slow, but I'll mend."

She was carefully rolling her left arm in a circle as Hope dried her hands on a towel and joined them. The young woman met their gazes with a little too much confidence, rocking on her heels. Naomi couldn't decide if the new nurse was forcing cheer or using it to hide something. Charles intertwined his fingers with Naomi's, as if wondering the same thing.

Hope drummed her fingers on her thighs and pursed her lips. "I want to preface what I'm about to tell you with a dose of grace, if you will. Hannah is a fine nursing assistant. If she chose to pursue a career in nursing, I have no doubt she would be a welcome addition to the medical field."

Charles lifted his chin and dropped a hand on his gun, his eyes narrowing with suspicion. "But?"

Hope took a deep breath. "Judging by your wounds, Naomi, you must have been covered head to toe in blood when they brought you to Hannah. To the untrained eye, blood and tissue, well," she shrugged, "it could be an easy assumption to make."

Naomi tilted her head. Hope was trying to protect Hannah from something. "Whatever you're dancing around, just say it. Hannah didn't sew my arm to my chest or anything, so whatever you don't want to say can't be that bad."

"You're still pregnant."

A pristine silence settled in the room, thicker and more perfect than any Naomi had ever experienced. Neither she nor Charles moved, breathed, spoke. Her mind froze.

"A little bleeding early in a pregnancy is not unusual. That, mixed with the wounds inflicted by the cat...this was an easy mistake to make." Hope smiled. "I hope it's good news to you and I hope Hannah won't be too hard on herself for the mistake. Please don't hold it against her."

Naomi needed to sit down. "And you're sure?"

"Very."

She staggered back and Charles helped her find the chair. "I'm pregnant." *I'm pregnant.* She couldn't seem to get the impact of the words. *I'm going to have a baby.* She looked up at Charles who knelt before her, still holding her hand. His dark, mischievous eyes shined, white teeth gleamed, such a contrast to his black beard and mustache. She leaned closer to him and tested the words. "I'm going to have a baby."

"A baby." He kissed her, kissed her again, and she sensed he was holding back giddy laughter. He pulled her to her feet and turned to Hope. "Thank you, Miss Clark. Please feel free to settle in as you see fit—with the understanding I am still intent on finding a doctor for Defiance. Especially now."

A soft knock on the door ended the appointment. "My next appointment."

Naomi smiled at Hope, the meager movement of muscle not expressing a fraction of her joy. "Thank you. Thank you for coming to Defiance."

~

The cat sunk his fangs into Naomi's neck and she screamed in agony. Claws that felt like bolts of lightning ripped open her back. He tried to pull her away from Charles—she reached for her husband and gasped at the sight of her bloody hand, flesh ripped away from her fingers.

A fog drifted between them and Charles faded from her sight, yet she knew he was still there. The cat bit down again, torturing, tormenting, the pain slicing her afresh. She was on the ground now, fighting. He growled demonically as he tore flesh from her forearms. Screaming for Charles, Naomi fought back, pounding the cougar in the face, trying to avoid his fangs, smearing her blood across his snout.

Suddenly, it wasn't the cat on top of her but Matthew and she froze, more afraid of him than the animal. He leered at her as he pinned her arms over her head. "You'll watch him die, too."

Her fear turned to rage. "No," she bellowed, "I won't let you hurt him. I won't—"

"Naomi, good God, wake up." Her heart hammering in her chest like a thundering herd of buffalo, gasping for breath, Naomi opened her eyes. Charles had an arm around her and grasped her face with his other hand. "It's all right. It was a dream." In the moonlight, she could see his eyes, wide with concern.

But he was all right. She touched his face, felt the prickle of his beard beneath her fingers. It had been a dream. Just a dream. Naomi melted into his chest and he wrapped her in a warm, safe hug. She forced her breathing and her heart to slow down. Just another nightmare.

"Were you dreaming about the cat again?"

"Yes—" and no. She could still feel Matthew on top of her and pressed closer into Charles. "These nightmares need to stop. They can't be good for the baby."

Charles chuckled softly. "She hung on through the attack. She may be tougher than you think."

"She?"

"I have no doubt, Naomi, you will give me a daughter." His gentle tone rang with light-hearted sarcasm.

She nuzzled his chest, everything right again in her world. "You might be surprised."

Yes, merely dreams. And they would pass in time.

Nine

THE IDEA TO buy the Sunnyside Mine wouldn't leave Matthew, even though a large Saturday night crowd in the saloon gave him hope for the town's fortunes. He surveyed the smoky room from the first landing on the staircase and reminded himself a healthy number of customers wasn't as good as outright-busting-at-the-seams. Like the Chandelier was used to.

He'd told the girls to stop entertaining customers for a week in an attempt to get that prig of a mayor Ian Donoghue off his back. Closing down one pastime had funneled a few more bodies here, but it was only a temporary solution. A poor one at that. Things needed to change in Defiance.

The town needed men.

Men wallowed in sin. Bred it. Demanded it. Thank God, couldn't live without it. Enough of the right men showing up in Defiance would swing the pendulum toward prosperity with the unstoppable force of an avalanche. Best of all, there wouldn't be a darn thing the sheriff, the mayor, or even Charles McIntyre could do about it.

And wouldn't it just frost Naomi for the town to turn back to the den of iniquity she'd wanted so desperately to get away from? So desperately, in fact, she'd asked Matthew to come rescue her and her sisters.

Only, he'd been a day late and a dollar short. Again. Losing her to a less-than-equal rival.

He shook his head, reminding himself to stop picking at an old wound and get back to the matter at hand.

The mine. It had to reopen.

McIntyre needed some kind of nudge. Something to move him, convince him to divest himself of the Sunnyside. Sell it and walk away, not merely sit on it. Matthew needed a plan to create the nudge.

He knew people back in California. People with money. A few of them so rich they could light their stoves with stacks of hundred dollar bills or stuff their mattresses with the cash.

Yes, that was a way to proceed. The idea blossomed in his brain like an ink spill. He'd send out some telegrams, see if maybe—

"Yeah, she's gonna have a baby. The little sister made a mistake."

Matthew's attention immediately shot to two men having a drink at the end of the bar, a few feet below him.

"Mighty big mistake," one observed.

"Mebbe so, but my wife heard the whole thing."

"Imagine *Charles McIntyre* with a baby," the flushed miner whispered too loudly. "Didn't think I'd ever see that."

"Might give him a better disposition."

"Might. I hear tell he's already going soft. A kid just might turn him sweet and all." The man took a swig of his beer and wiped away the foamy mustache. "I don't reckon it was meant for my wife's ears, though, so don't repeat it."

"She sure is a busybody." The other man lifted his beer toward his lips. "Anybody see her with her ear to the key hole?"

"Not this time." The two men had a hearty laugh and moved on to discussing the paltry amount of gold coming out of the creek.

Matthew's grip tightened so hard on the rail, he could feel the wood giving beneath his fingers. His jaw clenched with a herculean force.

A baby. The bastard stole Naomi from me and now they're going to start a family. That should be my baby...

Jealousy, dark, wretched, foul, writhed in his heart. *He's gotten everything he ever wanted. He's gotten everything I've ever wanted. But I came so close...once.*

Matthew had met Naomi on the street a few weeks back, right before the mountain lion had got hold of her. He'd attempted to chat. She'd merely smiled, said she was in a hurry, and pushed that half-breed son right past him. Matthew thought Christians were supposed to forgive.

And now she and McIntyre had a brat of their own coming into this world.

Matthew rubbed his temples, trying to massage out the darkness. But something in his brain writhed, strained, snapped.

No. No. NO!

He was done.

He'd had enough of losing. Losing to someone like his brother had been one thing. John had been a good man. Deserving of a woman like Naomi. But to lose her to Charles McIntyre—an infamous pimp—had been a nearly incapacitating blow. Now, they had a baby on the way?

Matthew'd had all he was going to take.

At that moment, he decided no matter what it cost him, no matter what steps he had to take, if he had to sell his soul to the very devil himself, he was going to break Charles McIntyre. Break him financially, spiritually, any way he could think of.

And make sure Naomi watched it all come undone.

Hannah dropped down hard in the chair near the stove. Hope clutched her shoulder, gave her a reassuring squeeze. "Please don't take this too hard, Hannah. You saved your sister's life. Therefore, you saved the baby's as well."

"But I told her—I said—my diagnosis—the blood—I was wrong. I was wrong." Hannah felt like she might be sick, so deep was her regret and humiliation.

"Calm down." Hope came round to face her. "The circumstances were quite stressful. And you had no one to turn to. No teacher. But you'll learn. I—and experience—will teach you. Eventually perhaps nursing school. You will learn." She nudged Hannah's chin up. "Focus on the two lives you *saved* and move forward. Can you do that?"

Hannah swallowed against the nausea rising in her stomach. Hope was right. Naomi was alive, and now, so, too, was the baby. *Oh, Lord, did I save their lives?* That would make the humiliation worth it.

"We have to move past this. There are patients coming in today."

Hannah rose slowly to her feet and smoothed her apron. "Then let's get ready for them."

And the patients came. Several a day. Hannah thought she was happier about it than Hope, as Hope was teaching her so much. Just today Hannah had learned some basic anatomy, pre-clinical procedures, and recognizing early signs of heart failure. Hope's methods were new, modern, her knowledge arguably as wide as Doc's. Perhaps even a little beyond.

Taking a whistling kettle off the stove, Hannah poured scalding water over a sink full of instruments. The last bit of washing before they closed the office for the evening. She returned the kettle to the stove as the door to examination room two opened.

"Take those twice a day," Hope was saying to a young man as she walked him to the door. Pale as a gravestone, he nodded slowly but attentively as she talked. "Don't miss a day. Two every day for five days, then come back and see me." She stopped at the threshold as he stepped out on to the porch. "And, from now on, cook your venison till the juices run clear."

"Yes, ma'am." He raised the bottle of stomach pills. "And thank you. Oh, how much do I owe you?"

"Um, let's say a dollar." The man fished some coins from his pants pocket, gave them to Hope and nodded his good-bye. She watched him for a moment, then shut the door. "My, this was a long day. I'm ready to put my feet up—"

A knock on the door stopped Hannah from answering. Hope puttered her lips in exhaustion, but opened the door again. "Yes, can I help you?"

"I need to see the doctor." A slender woman with sickly gray shadows under her eyes pushed past Hope and marched into the office. Her faded, low-cut dress and tinted red hair announced her vocation with certainty. "I'm not leaving till I do." She spotted Hannah in the corner at the sink and narrowed her eyes at her. "You're too young to be the doctor. Where's the doctor?"

Hope cleared her throat and shut the door. "I'm the—I mean, I am—you see, um, there is no doctor here, but I am a very competent nurse. I'm sure I can help you."

The woman appraised her with a suspicious stare and

pursed lips. Pushing frizzy hair off her forehead, she raised her chin. "I need rid of the baby I'm carrying. I can pay. I've got cash."

Hannah gasped and Hope's mouth fell open. "By 'rid of,'" Hope spoke carefully, "do you mean you want to abort your pregnancy?"

"My money's good. Here." She raised her arm to display a worn, beaded reticule hanging from her wrist. "I always try to go to either a real doctor or a real nurse. No shysters."

"Always..." Hope faded off. "How many times—?" She bit that off and started again. "I'm a doc—I mean, a nurse. I can't take a life. I took a vow to only save lives."

The woman sniffed and appraised Hope with a curled lip. "What's your price?"

"I said I don't perform abortions. The money has nothing to do with it, I'm sorry. I can help you deliver the baby."

Hannah stepped forward quickly. "Have it and you can give it up for adoption."

The woman cut narrowed, storming eyes at her. "Oh, yeah, I know you. You knocked on my tent once. You and Mollie. Invited me to church. Well, the only thing I'm interested in saving is my waistline and my income."

The callousness of the woman's words hit Hannah like a slap. How lost and blind was a person to believe a baby could be discarded like dirty bathwater? A baby... Oh, God, open this woman's eyes. Soften her heart. Don't let her kill a child.

"I'd be happy to examine you," Hope said, "give you some prenatal care, but abortion is out of the question."

"Pre-na—what?"

"Monitor you. Keep you healthy for the pregnancy. Deliver the baby when the time comes. Help you through the entire process."

The woman snorted in disgust. "That sounds like a racket,

for sure. No, I ain't having this baby. If you won't rid me of it,
I'll find someone who will."

"There is no other trained nurse in town," Hannah added
in a rush, hoping the argument might give the woman pause.

"Oh, there's somebody. There's always somebody."

She turned to go but Hope clutched her elbow. "Please
don't do this. It could be dangerous for you."

For a moment, Hannah saw a softening in the woman's
hard features. A sad expression tugged at the corners of her
mouth. "I can't bring a child into my world. If I die, maybe
that's the best outcome."

Speechless, heartbroken, Hannah prayed for the woman as
she slipped out the door.

"If I don't help her, she could die," Hope whispered, staring
down at her hands twisting in her apron.

"If you do help her, a child *will* die. Could you live with
that?"

Hope didn't answer her.

Ten

⁓

SEVERAL DAYS LATER, a young black woman came pounding on Hope's door in the middle of the night. Someone in Tent Town needed help. Now, she scurried ahead on the dark path, illuminated here and there by the amber glow of tents, as Hope scrambled to keep up, holding her medical bag in a death grip.

Shortly, the girl stopped at a tent and jerked her chin toward it. "She's in there. Been a mess since yesterday morning. I'm two tents down if you need me."

"Actually, yes, I need you to go fetch Hannah Frink. She lives at the hotel."

"I don't want—"

"Or you can stay and assist."

The girl made an offended huffing noise but headed off toward main street.

Hope ducked into the tent and found the woman from the other day—the one who had practically demanded an abortion—lying on her cot, groaning, drenched in sweat. Hope lifted the covers and grimaced at the blood-soaked nightgown.

Suspecting the reason for a call from a soiled dove at this hour, she had come prepared with various tinctures and menstrual cloths. After an examination, Hope suspected a tear in the cervix, possibly one in the uterus as well. She administered asphenamine and quinine, pressed in bandages, and waited for Hannah to help her move the patient.

The woman moaned softly. Sweat glistened on her forehead and drenched her ruby hair. Her pulse was weak and thready. Whoever she'd found to perform the abortion had been nothing short of a butcher and Hope was seriously concerned.

"I'm here." Hannah said, rushing into the tent. She grimaced at the pale, sweaty woman, but recovered quickly. "I brought our wagon. In case."

Guilt and fear squeezed in on Hope. "Good. The bleeding is too heavy. If her uterus has been punctured, surgery may be the only way to save her."

"Surgery?"

"But in these primitive conditions it could kill her. She's already lost too much blood. She is in a weakened state. The fever is evidence of infection."

"It sounds like she is dying," Hannah said softly, shock in her tone.

"Yes."

"If you don't do surgery, what else can you do?"

"Wait." Which was the same as saying *nothing*. Her stomach twisted. If only the bleeding would stop on its own. *If only she'd sent for me sooner...* "I have to move her to the office," she muttered, thinking out loud but aware of Hannah. "Help me get her in the wagon."

～

A change came over Hope that Hannah had seen once before—in the restaurant when she'd saved Mr. Ledford. Here in the office, with the patient resting on the table and ready for surgery, Hope stood straighter, her voice became more authoritative, her hands moved with skill and confidence as she wielded the scalpel.

In spite of the dire situation, Hannah was fascinated by the peek at the inside of the female reproductive organs. Hope narrated under her breath, explaining anatomical references like the anterior superior iliac spines, the subcutaneous fat and rectus sheath, entry into the peritoneal cavity, on and on.

Hannah had assisted Doc with enough minor surgeries to know one thing: something about this patient wasn't right. Her flesh was too pale. Her heartbeat too slow. The loss of blood was possibly too much to overcome, never mind the trauma of the surgery.

But Hope worked calmly with focus and determination. Hannah dabbed the woman's forehead with a towel—the sweat there the only indication Hope was under pressure.

"There it is, there's the puncture. Get me the iron."

Hannah rushed over to the stove and plucked a small cauterizing iron with a rosewood handle from the fire. The wood was warm, but manageable. She rushed it back over to Hope who pressed the tip to the wound. The scent of burning flesh filled Hannah's nostrils and she had to force down the urge to vomit. "All right." Hope laid the instrument on the counter. "Let's close her."

Hannah swung around to the tray of medical implements beside the iron and picked up the threaded, crescent-shaped needle. As Hope sutured the wound, Hannah deflated a little, overwhelmed with all there would be to learn in a real nursing school.

"I can see why you were top of your class. I had no idea nursing schools taught this—taught surgery."

Hope swallowed, paused for an instant, then kept going. "Yes, nursing school. You'd be surprised what they teach you now."

"It was very demanding, I suppose?"

"Very."

"Did you think Defiance would present such a challenge?"

Hope extended a waiting hand. "Scissors." Hannah responded and Hope cut the thread. "Honestly, I didn't know what to expect."

"You've truly been called to nursing. I can see God's hand in everything you do." Again Hannah caught a pause, a stutter, as if Hope was debating what to say and in the end said nothing. "I think you might be more gifted with a scalpel than Doc—" An idea, a crazy, irrational thought struck Hannah and she peered intently at Hope.

Hope leaned in to inspect her finished stitches one by one, but seemed to sense Hannah's gaze. "What?"

No. That was a crazy idea. Why would she lie? She had the references, and clearly a medical background. But what kind of medical background exactly? "You're so skilled. Almost like a doctor."

"Yes," Hope said, standing up. "Almost like. Now, let's get everything cleaned up."

~

"I don't know, Billy. I can't put my finger on it." Hannah toddled along the aisle of the mercantile, helping their son practice walking. Little Billy gripped her index fingers and swaggered drunkenly between the canned tomatoes on one side and barrels of flour on the other.

"Try," he said, without looking up from the ledger he was working on at the counter. "Fumbling for words might help you figure out what bothers you about her."

"It doesn't bother me. That's not the right word. I just get this sense she's holding back or..."

"Hiding something?"

"Maybe, but that makes it sound bad. I don't think it is. She's just a very private person."

"Could she be running from something or someone?"

"She mentioned a man. He didn't stick with her. He didn't want her to be a nurse."

Billy's eyes did come up at that. "Then he was a fool and she's better off without him."

Hannah's heart swelled. Billy believed in her. He made her think she could be a nurse—one as well trained as Hope. And he was even willing to uproot their lives. "Maybe she's trying to get over the heartbreak by coming to Defiance—someplace remote and adventurous."

Billy chuckled. "If she wanted adventurous, she should have come when Delilah was at the height of her chaos."

Her back beginning to ache from stooping over, she set her son down on his rear end and straightened for a good stretch. Yes, only a few months ago Defiance had been a den of wild debauchery and shamelessness. Delilah and her Crystal Chandelier had risen from the ground like a hungry demon singing a siren's song. Then that awful man had sabotaged the mine, blowing it sky high, burying twelve men beneath tons of rock.

Maybe the town with them.

"Charles thinks Defiance is bouncing back," she said, lacing her words with optimism she didn't quite feel.

"He and I have talked about it. The town can grow, but the pace will be slower without the mine."

"Not the most attractive place for a world-class doctor to

come, but Charles is convinced he'll find one. In the meantime, Hope is the most skilled nurse I've ever seen. You wouldn't believe the surgery she performed this morning. Did I tell you—?"

"Twice. You told me twice."

She laughed and swept Little Billy up into her arms. "Well, I'm out of stories then, little man. How about you and me go back to the hotel and get us some lunch? Are you hungry?"

"Howy," Little Billy said, grinning. "Howy."

"Oh, listen to you talking!" She slathered his little cherubic face with excited kisses. "I'm so proud of you, little man."

"Howy," the toddler said again, grinning.

Billy shook his head and came out from behind the counter. "He's growing so fast." He ruffled his son's downy blond hair, but the joyous smile faded and he narrowed his eyes at Hannah. "You're still sure?"

"I wish you'd quit asking me. I don't want anything more than for us to be a family."

"What about nursing school?"

She wanted to go more than ever because she'd made such a colossal mistake with Naomi's diagnosis. Her confidence hung in tatters, yet formal training would prevent future blunders. "I'm still not sure. I need to wait."

"On what?"

"Something in my spirit says sit tight. I can't tell you any more than that." She could hardly believe she still wanted to be a nurse but the dream wouldn't die. Could she—could Hannah —become a nurse like Hope?

Or dare she dream of something even bigger?

"Maybe working with Hope will help you find your focus."

Hannah blinked. No, this was not the time to share such a crazy thought. She had to pray about it. Wait for clear direction. Sit tight. "I've already learned it'll be far more work than I suspected. I don't know why she didn't go on to medical schoo—"

And the other crazy notion returned.

"What?" Billy asked.

"I wonder if she did try to go medical school. If she was rejected or failed? Or maybe that was the plan the young man didn't agree with. Maybe he thought nursing school should have been sufficient."

"Hannah." Billy laid a hand on her shoulder, she knew, to calm her racing mind. "This is all conjecture. Simply ask the woman."

Eleven

"IT'S MORE THAN FAIR, I will say." Charles could not dismiss an offer on the mine out of hand, not without sharing it with his partner, Ian. He slid it across the desk to the Scotsman with the grudging compliment.

"Let's have a look then." Ian pulled his spectacles from his sweater's collar and worked into them.

As he read over the business proposition, Charles smiled at his friend's belly which had become more noticeable as of late. The argyle sweater he wore did not hide it, and Ian's beard had turned completely gray. He was aging comfortably, as he had hoped to do, surrounded by Rebecca and her sisters.

To Charles, Ian was more than a friend and a business partner. He was also his brother-in-law, a label that epitomized the myriad changes he, Ian, and the town had gone through in the last few years. Some made him smile, some made him sick.

"'Tis a fair offer," Ian said. "I find that almost surprising. Have you ever heard of this..." he carefully read the company name aloud, "MP&G Western Mining Conglomerate? And what of the members listed here?"

"The Board of Directors. Charles Crocker and Allan Ladd are quite wealthy. Crocker is a railroad man. Ladd made his fortune in the gold rush and invested wisely. I am not familiar with the other two gentlemen."

Ian returned the paper and settled back, crossing a leg over one knee. "As I've said, I think we should sell it. This is a good offer. It would rid ye of the albatross the mine has become to ye. Ye'd be flush with capital. Ye could focus on the spur line."

Charles sighed heavily. "What if the mine is reopened and another accident happens? More men die?"

Ian laced his fingers over his paunch and pursed his lips. "I understand yer concern for the men who work the mines. It is admirable. Ye tried to make the mine as safe as ye could. But what happened could not have been foreseen. The catastrophe perpetrated by Delilah was more the fault of a broken, vengeful heart than a lapse in safety standards."

"Yes, I guess that's fair. She and Logan seemed destined for tragedy."

"Aye. Ye know, Scripture says every man shall bear his own burden. Yers is enough for ye. Ye need to quit trying to bear everyone else's as well."

"Perhaps." He shook his head, putting the offer aside for the moment. "Regarding the spur line and getting the lumber milled. I've no desire to send our wood to Matthew's sawmill. I think I will buy it."

"What if he won't sell it to ye?"

"Then I will build my own."

Ian nodded. "Ye've got several men working for ye with experience enough to manage one. Either way, it would be unwise to allow him to become a bottleneck for ye."

"Exactly my thinking. I don't trust him. We need to insure ourselves against any dependency on his lumberyard."

"Anything else?" Ian patted his stomach. "Rebecca is meeting me at the hotel for lunch."

"It does my heart good to see you so happy. There is nothing more important than family."

Ian's face fell. A pinch between his gray brows expressed his sympathy. "Again, I'm sorry for yer loss. If ye need anything, ye know Rebecca and I are here for ye."

"We may be calling upon you for nanny services." Charles tried and failed to keep a foolish grin from betraying his news.

Ian regarded him with a mix of confusion and amusement. "Lad, ye're trying to tell me something but I'm not tracking."

"A moment ago I was thinking you are a friend, a mentor, a business partner, a brother-in-law. There is one more label we can hang on you, though."

"Aye, what's that?"

"Uncle."

~

A cup of coffee pressed to her lips, Rebecca watched Hannah drizzle molasses over a steaming biscuit, tear off tiny pieces and feed them to Little Billy. Her glassy stare, however, said her mind was elsewhere. Around them, the Trinity Inn's restaurant reverberated with chatting customers, tinkling silverware, and the clank of dishes.

"Billy thinks I should just ask her outright."

Rebecca set the cup down. "Why don't you?"

"Oh, I suppose, eventually I will. I just thought by now she would have revealed a little more of her story to me."

"You said she's a private person. Those kind don't open up easily."

"I guess. It's just that sometimes when she talks, it's like she's saying one thing but thinking another. I don't know." She picked up a napkin and dabbed at her son's face. "I can't explain it."

"Awkward pauses? Sentences that seem to redirect abruptly?"

Hannah looked up. "Yes."

Rebecca nodded. "When I interviewed her, I had that same sense. As if she almost says one thing, but then quickly corrects and says something else."

"So, what do you think? Do you agree with me that something's amiss? But not necessarily something terrible," Hannah was quick to add.

"Possibly."

"I think it has something to do with her fiancé."

"This is all conjecture." Rebecca took another sip then grasped the cup in both hands. "Pointless speculation until..."

"Until what?"

"Until I actually do a little digging."

"Well, good morning, ladies."

Rebecca and Hannah looked up into Mollie's face. Her blue eyes twinkled and her cheeks were a healthy shade of rose. She was wearing her hair differently now, as well. Piled on her head in a French twist with several long, golden curls trailing down her back. The style made her look more mature.

"There's my favorite man." The girl bent down and smacked a wet raspberry on Little Billy's cheeks. The child rolled with hysterical giggles.

She's glowing, Rebecca thought, and grinned. She knew the look. She'd seen it on Hannah and Naomi. Even herself. Love painted hearts with an unmistakable hue. "Good morning, Mollie. You look beautiful."

"Oh," Hannah snapped her fingers, "I forgot to tell you, Rebecca." She reached across the table and tagged her sister's arm. "Billy just promoted Mollie to dining room manager."

Mollie straightened up and the glow coming from her brightened exponentially. "Yes. Yes, he did."

"Oh, that's wonderful." Rebecca was truly happy for the girl. "You'll be running the whole hotel before we know it."

Mollie winked. "That's the plan."

Hannah chuckled. "And I'll see a little more of the man I'm supposed to be marrying. What did Emilio say?"

"Oh, I haven't seen him yet to tell him. Probably see him tonight."

Hannah clutched Mollie's hand and squeezed excitedly. "I'm sure he'll be thrilled for you. For you both, if there's any kind of future planning going on."

The pink in Mollie's cheeks spread up her face and down into her white, cotton shirt. "No, no. We're just both, um," she cast about as if looking for a chore, "Well, I've got some inventory to check. Have a nice day, girls."

She strode off in a hurry, leaving Rebecca and Hannah laughing, but the humor seemed to die suddenly in Hannah. Rebecca didn't miss the abrupt fade. "Honey, are you jealous?"

Hannah's eye bugged. "No. Heavens no. I just had a moment of...missing Emilio's company. Or, really, missing the way things were. We were all so close when we lived in the hotel."

Rebecca smiled, a little sadly. "Those were good days, but they weren't meant to last forever. Life moves on. Naomi's happy out on her great, big, rolling ranch. I love Ian and we both enjoy running the newspaper. You and Billy, Emilio, Mollie, you'll all find your path."

"You're right, I know. I just hope we all don't drift too far apart."

"Well, we can keep working on one reason to gather together." Rebecca bit her lip and winked. "Let's finish the details for your wedding."

At first Hannah looked a touched perplexed, then her expression softened. "He loves me and he wants me to be happy."

Rebecca was gratified to agree. "Yes. Turns out, Billy Page is a good man. I would have never put money on it, but your love brought out the best in him."

Twelve

THE RATTLE of a buggy pulled Naomi's and Emilio's attention from the horse he was saddling in the barn and they both peered up the road. "It's Hannah," she said, stepping outside to see better. Her sister was riding with Billy, holding Little Billy between them.

A sense of relief washed over Naomi. She was eager to see her little sister and had been trying to get to town. Gathering here at the ranch was much better. She could only assume the misdiagnosis of the baby was hanging over Hannah and Naomi was desperate to share her joy—not any blame.

Emilio tested the cinch on Buttercup's saddle then flipped the stirrup in place. "You're all set, Señora Naomi. Can I help you into the saddle?"

"I don't suppose I should turn down the help. I'm still pretty stiff."

Determined not to let her wounds hold her back, Naomi climbed into the saddle, with a little boost from Emilio. Moving like an old woman, holding her left arm pressed to her side, she managed to get her seat.

The brim of Emilio's cowboy hat did not hide the deep crease in his brow. He looked decidedly uncertain about this ride. "Are you sure—?"

"I will not be bedridden. And now it looks like I won't be going far anyway. Thank you for your help." She winked at him. "I won't breathe a word to Charles if you don't."

Biting his bottom lip, he nodded and stepped back from the horse. "Sí."

Naomi took a deep breath, squeezed her thighs against Buttercup's sides and *tsked.* The horse moved and quickly they worked up from a jog that tweaked every former stitch with pain to a lope as smooth as a rocking chair.

It came to an end too quickly. "Well, what a nice surprise." She reined in her horse alongside Hannah, the transition jarring every wound. "What brings y'all out this way?"

"Should you be riding?" her sister asked, disapproval evident in her scowl.

Ever the nurse, Naomi thought. "I'm not going jumping. I'm careful."

"Charles sent for me, Naomi." Billy pulled back on the reins, slowing the team. "He around?"

"No, he hasn't come back from the lumber camp yet."

"Well, we're a little early. We can wait."

"Mollie's watching the store for us so we decided to make an afternoon of the visit." Hannah shifted Little Billy on to her lap so the boy could see better. "Can you blow Aunt Naomi a kiss?" Obediently he performed his new trick with pudgy fingers and Naomi's heart melted.

She nudged her horse closer and leaned over to ruffle the little man's hair. The exertion caused every wound to smart in protest, but she grit her teeth against the pain. "Oh, I love your kisses. You've made me so happy!" Her heart full of joy, she straightened up and simply endured the pain. "Billy, why don't you go fetch Charles? You can take Buttercup here. Hannah, we can talk over some coffee."

Billy set the brake. "Sounds like a fine idea. Girl talk while I go find the King rancher."

On the way into the house, Naomi paused on the porch and looked out at the ranch. Spread out around them, a valley of grass turning amber for fall accommodated two thousand head of cattle. Cowboys whooped and hollered, their every move stalked by a dust cloud. Down by the river, a forest of Aspens quivered in the breeze, golden leaves fluttering to earth. Above it all, the snow-capped San Juan Mountains watched over them in majestic silence. Ever since the cougar attack, she'd found herself stopping to appreciate this view over and over. And it was even better from the back porch.

"You'll never get tired of this will you?"

Puzzled, Naomi looked over at her sister. "Tired of what?"

"The wide open spaces, the freedom, the fresh air. Charles. It's all over your face."

Naomi let an embarrassed grin break. "I am pretty happy. And I won't take any of it for granted now. Not even a single breath."

Hannah shuddered. "The bite on your shoulder was meant for your neck. He could have—"

"But he didn't," Naomi interrupted. "I'm looking at the good, not the bad. God was with me. Watching over me, strengthening me."

"Are you still having the nightmares?"

"No, at least, not every night now, but..."

"But what?"

Naomi let her gaze drift back out over the wide, sweeping valley she called home. "I dreamed about our son." She patted her stomach protectively. "He was tall, dark like Charles. A teenager in the dream." She smiled in spite of the knot forming in her throat. "And he was riding Bullet at a wide-open gallop across the field there. He dipped down between the hills...I lost sight of him." She paused, remembering what about this dream disturbed her. "Then he reappeared, only it wasn't him. It was Matthew. And I was terrified of him."

"Just because it was a scary dream, it doesn't mean—"

"Anything? I suppose, but it's happened before, my dreams turning into him. I guess in my mind he represents evil." She tugged on Hannah's sleeve. "Let's go brew a pot."

A few minutes later they were seated by the fire, holding cups of coffee and watching Little Billy scoot around on the rug, pushing a toy train and making train noises.

"Chug, chug, chug—Chooo-chooo."

Hannah smiled and turned her attention to Naomi. "I will say, Uncle Matthew sure has turned into something I don't recognize."

Naomi wrapped all ten fingers around her warm mug, dispelling a sudden chill, in spite of the fire. "I will not worry about him today. I am blessed beyond measure and there's certainly nothing he can do to change that."

"Yes," Hannah's face fell. "Speaking of blessings—"

"Hannah, I know you want to apologize, but don't bother." Naomi reached out and clutched her sister's free hand. "I'm going to have a baby. You probably saved him because you saved me—"

"But what if I'd administered the wr—"

"There are no what-ifs. Can't you see that? God used you with the knowledge you had. You saved us. Nothing else matters, Hannah. Nothing."

Hannah pulled away, taking a sip of coffee to hide blinking back tears. "We have a patient in town. A woman who nearly died from a botched abortion. She actually came and asked Hope to perform it."

Naomi had to bite back a knee-jerk and very unkind response about the woman. But she did manage, "A prostitute?" The question itself was loaded with judgment.

Hannah nodded. "And she talked like this wasn't her first. She was so callous and so, I don't know, detached. The baby was a problem, an inconvenience. Not a human." She shook her head and exhaled a long, slow breath. "Chilling. It's just chilling someone could be that blind to the truth."

"I assume the baby died?"

Hannah nodded and Naomi again had to work to tame her tongue.

"I look at her and then us," Hannah continued. "The difference in the way we view life is astonishing. She would throw away a baby. You would do anything to have one. I would do anything to save one, especially yours."

"I know." Naomi set her coffee on the table beside her chair, the drink upsetting her stomach. A common occurrence lately. "I know, too, you'll take good care of me and your new nephew when he arrives."

"I will. And Hope will. I swanny, she's as good as a doctor. I don't think Charles knows how blessed we are to have her."

"I think he appreciates her, he's simply adamant about getting a doctor to Defiance. And I do mean adamant. He's placed ads in newspapers across the country."

"She's so skilled, I—I, well, I find her very inspiring."

Naomi tilted her head, waiting for the explanation of what Hannah *wasn't* saying.

Her little sister twisted in obvious discomfort. "Billy thinks I'm being so *patient* about the wedding because I might really want to go to nursing school."

"Don't you?"

"On the one hand, I don't think I'm worthy. On the other..." Hannah narrowed her eyes at Naomi and leaned forward a little. "What if I wanted more? How would you feel about that?"

"More than nursing school?"

"What if I wanted to be a doctor?"

"A doctor?" Naomi had not meant to scoff, but a hint of it raced out with her shock, and Hannah's face fell. Naomi berated herself for the slip up, but still... "You're serious? You want to be a doctor?"

Hannah rose and wandered a few feet away, her back to Naomi. "I'm so amazed by Hope's skills and it's obvious she could do more, be more. She makes it seem possible and there *are* a few female doctors in the country."

Naomi took a deep breath and laced her fingers together in her lap. "Well..." *That's a lot to think about.* She decided to say so. "Have you considered what you'd have to give up, how hard it would be, the amount of studying you'd have to do?"

Hannah didn't answer right away. After a long silence, she finally said, "I could do it."

"I have no doubt." Naomi rose and stood closer to the fire, her back to Hannah. "But the sacrifice. Women have to give up so much to pursue careers."

"But if you got hurt again, or if anyone I love got hurt again, think what a difference that training could make."

"Well, I think you've done a wonderful job saving lives with what little training you've had." An idea dawned on Naomi and she turned to Hannah. "You're not responsible for saving the world. You know that, right?"

Hannah shrugged a shoulder then frowned. "You don't think a woman should be a doctor?"

"What? I didn't say that."

"The sacrifices. The choices. Wife. Mother. Doctor. Either. Or."

"I don't think it's necessarily either-or, but God did make us different from men. We have different concerns and needs. Different abilities suited better to certain tasks. Generally speaking, we tend to be more emotional. Doctors need to have a certain amount of stoicism—"

"We're not as stable as men." Hannah rose as well. Anger had crept into her voice. "You don't think a woman should be a doctor."

"Stop putting words in my mouth. I never said that."

"Then what are you saying?"

Naomi took a breath to clamp down on her own irritation before speaking again. "We just have to make choices that men don't. How to raise our children if we have careers, for one. I just think you sh—" She bit that off. Hannah was not in the mood to be bossed. "I hope you ponder carefully what you might have to give up and what you really want out of life. I mean, think hard."

Thirteen

NAOMI ALMOST FAILED to stifle a bored yawn. Leo LeBeaux was a fine lay preacher but the little Frenchman didn't preach with as much fire as Logan had. She missed the former gunfighter's passion in the pulpit. She also found it difficult not to be distracted by LeBeaux's ears. Large and always pink, as if the man was flushed, they stuck out more than the average set.

Frustrated with her mental rabbit trails, she shifted slightly on the hard pew and lamented the fact that LeBeaux also preached much longer than Logan had. How odd he took more time to say less.

Oh, she was just being petulant. Logan had been able to stir her soul with his heartfelt sermons. LeBeaux had a heart to preach and was learning the skill of oration. They could be patient.

However, a glance to her left at Charles and to her right at Two Spears, confirmed her suspicions. The blank, bored expressions on their faces said they missed Logan, too.

Mercifully, a few moments later, LeBeaux wrapped up his sermon on pride. Amid friendly banter, handshakes, and smiles, the congregation spilled out onto the porch. A cool day, the sky spit intermittent drops of rain at them.

Pulling her cape tighter, Naomi paused to consider Tent Town. It had changed, but only in the number of sinners. The traffic was lighter on Sundays, but clearly some of the men passing by were intoxicated, as denoted by their staggering gaits. A few women with clothes baskets on their hips tossed haughty glances at the church as they headed for the creek. Somewhere on the other side of a row of tents, the rising volume of two men arguing peppered the air with profane insults.

As Naomi and Charles stood discussing supper plans with Rebecca, Ian, Hannah, and Billy, a frail woman wearing a baleful glare, pushed between Mollie and Emilio, working surprised expression from them, and climbed the three steps to the porch. Her bloodshot eyes bored into Charles as she strode straight up to him and summarily slapped him across the face. The sound echoed down the street like a rifle shot. Naomi gasped as the group surged forward as if to protect Charles. Charles didn't move. Didn't raise a hand to his cheek. His expression didn't even change.

"My husband is dead because of you. He died in that hell-hole you called a mine."

"How dare you?" Naomi took a step forward, but Charles subtly waved her off.

"Let her say what's on her mind. Maybe it will give her some peace."

"The only thing that will ever give me peace is to see you hang for the deaths of all those men." The woman's bony chin quivered with her pain. "You and Delilah."

Charles' jaw clenched. Naomi saw his throat move but still he didn't respond to the ugly accusation. His family and friends gawked at the grieving wife, but kept their silence.

"I'll take your money," she continued, "only because of my boys. But it don't buy my forgiveness."

LeBeaux slowly pushed through the congregants and faced the woman, positioning himself between her and Charles. "I am sorry for your loss, but this man is not responsible for your husband's death. And no anger, no vengeance, will return your beloved to you. You must offer forgiveness so that your wounds over this loss will heal."

The woman's eyes widened as if she couldn't believe the suggestion. "Forgive him?" She cut her eyes at Charles, and Naomi's soul recoiled at the hate she saw burning in them. "I don't have a husband. My children don't have a father. I have to leave my home because I can't afford to keep it. Forgive you? I'd like to cut out your heart."

No one said anything. The silence laid on them like a cold winter fog. Her eyes spilling tears, the woman spun and raced back down the street.

Naomi, hurting for her husband, slipped her hand into his. Every line, every muscle in his face looked brittle, like ice—a thin veneer barely hiding his pain. He had paled, the contrast between his white skin and the dark beard and eyes jarring.

"She didn't mean any of that, Charles. She's just grieving."

"The mine was as safe as a mine can be," Ian said firmly. "It was never meant to handle an explosion of dynamite. The collapse was no one's fault but Delilah's and Smith's."

Charles sighed, but didn't say anything. His gaze stayed riveted on the woman.

Assuming the last thing her husband wanted now was a large family gathering, Naomi turned to Rebecca. "I think we'll excuse ourselves from Sunday supper."

. . .

They were halfway home before Naomi finally decided to speak, prompted by the perplexed expression on Two Spear's face in the back of the buggy. She laid a hand on Charles' thigh and said softly, "You can't keep blaming yourself. You shouldn't blame yourself at all."

"I own the mine."

"Exactly. You own it. You didn't dig the tunnels yourself. You didn't hire every single miner yourself. You certainly didn't tell Delilah to blow it up. People make their own decisions, Charles."

"The fund I set up for the widows and orphans—she took the money. All of them did. Still, there is so much hate."

"They're grieving. They need time. The money you gave them at least takes a few worries off their minds. One day, I think they'll be able to see that...and your heart. One day, we'll all be past this."

He leaned forward, resting his elbows on his knees, the reins loose in his hands, his shoulders riding high with tension. "One day."

Naomi tried to squelch her irritation but her husband wasn't acting like himself. "What's the matter with you? The old Charles McIntyre wouldn't have given a nickle about those men and their families. The new Charles McIntyre has turned himself into a whipping boy."

Charles sat up abruptly, opened his mouth to argue, she presumed, but his eyes darted back to Two Spears and he bit back whatever he was about to say.

Naomi softened her voice. "The deaths of those men are not on your head."

"Someone has to suffer for what happened."

She let out a long, exasperated breath. "Someone already did. On a cross."

Monday after lunch, Hannah left Little Billy with his father and headed to the doctor's office, planning to spend the afternoon with Hope. With two patients in recovery, she wondered if she should offer to work some kind of regular schedule for the next few days, something Hope could plan on.

She let herself into the office, found the sitting area empty, but heard a bed squeak in examination room one. Where they had put the soiled dove. Hannah peeked through the crack in the door and was disturbed to find Hope sitting on the patient's bed, fingers pressed to her forehead, eyes closed.

"Hope?"

Slowly, she lifted her gaze to Hannah. Puzzled when she didn't say anything, Hannah looked past her to the patient. For a moment Hannah thought she had passed, but then her chest moved—a small motion. She was barely alive.

She sighed sadly and stepped into the room. "Is she going to make it?"

"I don't know."

"The surgery was flawless. If she doesn't make it, it's not your fault." Hannah stepped over to the woman and touched her hand lightly, whispering a prayer for healing.

"I don't even know her name."

"I'll try to find out."

"If she'd just given me a chance sooner." Hope stood up and moved as if she were carrying the world on her shoulders. "How is this going to look if she dies? The new doctor losing a patient?"

Hannah searched her friend's drawn face. "Doctor?" And she knew, with inexplicable certainty, she knew. "Doctor," she said firmly.

Yet, Hope tried to deny it. "Did I say doctor? I meant nurse, of course." She turned sideways as if to slide past Hannah, but Hannah blocked her.

"You *are* a doctor, aren't you? Why lie? Why pretend to be a nurse? Did you do something wrong? Did someone else die?"

Hope stepped back. "I assure you I am a very capable nurse."

"Then tell me the truth."

Hope hung her head. Debating, Hannah assumed, and therefore didn't rush her. The woman glanced back at the sleeping—dying?—patient. "In Denver, the women's group ran me out. Said a female doctor upset the balance, so to speak. That I would have their husbands expecting them to bear children *and* become lawyers and bankers as well. An unacceptable disruption to the status quo."

"That's awful."

"Yes, and foolish and ignorant. I have a gift. I can heal people. They should have left me alone." She sniffed and lifted her chin. "Please don't tell anyone. Especially Mr. McIntyre. Not yet. I need a chance to prove myself."

"He wouldn't run you out because you're a woman."

"How would Naomi react? I believe she thinks I am a competent nurse. Would she consider me to be as competent a doctor?"

Hannah thought back to her own conversation with Naomi.

Hope snorted. "I see it on your face."

"No, no, you don't understand. And I know my sister. If she knew you were a doctor, she'd think you're every bit as capable doing either. Every bit as capable as a man."

"You think so, do you?"

"Yes. Yes, I do. She's been very encouraging about my aspirations." If not a little shocked. And maybe a touch hesitant, truth be told.

"Because nursing is primarily a woman's field. Tell her you want to be a doctor and see if her attitude changes."

"I'm sure it wouldn't." Her voice lacked conviction. Naomi had expressed doubts, but only about Hannah and her goals, not about her potential skill or giftedness. Hope, on the other hand, had already achieved her medical license. "You have a gift from God. My sisters would expect you to use it."

"God." It seemed it took some effort for Hope not to sneer. "I don't know what God expects, but people have very definite expectations of what women can and should do. Often the expectations seem to clash."

Hannah wanted to ask Hope about her distance from God, but decided this wasn't the time. "You want me to hold my peace?"

Hope looked down and fidgeted with her own fingernails. "Yes. If you would. I will tell Mr. McIntyre and Naomi. I just need a little more time." She glanced back over her shoulder at the patient in the bed.

Arms loaded with a box of canned tomatoes, Billy emerged from the back room of the mercantile and drew to an abrupt halt. Hannah was leaning on the counter, twirling a lock of her pony tail around her finger, studying a medical book Hope had loaned her. Beside it lay the Montgomery Ward catalog opened to wedding dresses.

The juxtaposition of the choices was glaring and made Billy uneasy. He would move wherever Hannah needed to, to go to nursing school. He had meant that when he said it. He believed Hannah could have both—a nursing career and a family. If he believed it, surely she did.

Didn't she? Did she think she had to choose between family

and career? He walked up and gently set the box on the counter. "Are you pondering Chantilly lace or setting broken bones?"

Startled, she stood up. "Oh, well, at the moment, compression fractures to the spine, but," she swiped up the catalog as if to convince him the gowns were important as well, "I've already ordered a gown. You can't see it." She pressed the catalog to her chest.

Billy pondered the news. "I'm glad to hear it. And I know you'll be beautiful in whichever one you get." He decided to test a theory. "What have you learned about compression fractures? What are they?"

Her face lit up and her enthusiasm bubbled over as she explained the injury. "They're fractures that occur when a break collapses one or more vertebrae of the spine. They are linked to osteoporosis or thinning of the bone tissue. It is most often seen in the elderly and the infirm."

Billy's heart sank. Taken aback by the sudden change, he turned to the case of tomatoes. Tomatoes. He was happy here in this small town among friends and family, running a hotel and a mercantile.

Would that life be a prison for Hannah? Would small town life be enough if she came back here as a nurse?

"Billy, what's the matter?"

He hadn't meant to show anything, but they were only weeks away from the wedding. Married. A life commitment. "You have to search your heart, Hannah. You have to make some choices." He turned to her. "I want to be a part of your life, but I won't be an anchor, something that holds you back, drags you down. What do you want out of life? Is it here? With me?"

Hannah deflated as if she'd been called an ugly name. "Why are you even asking me these questions?"

"The change in you from talking about the dress to talking

about compression fractures was like night and day. Maybe we should postpone the wedding again."

Her mouth fell open. Billy couldn't believe he'd offered up the idea, but maybe they both needed a little time to figure out their future plans and goals. *God, what would I do if I lost her?*

He took her hand, to reassure her and himself. "I love you more than the air I breathe, and I believe you love me." He touched her cheek. "Which is why I can say with everything in me, I want you to be happy. I also thought we had things figured out, but maybe we don't." Hannah started to argue, he knew, but he raised a hand to her lips. "Think about what you want, Hannah. We'll talk about it at dinner tonight."

~

Charles laid his hand on the plaque imbedded on the mountain near the mine entrance and closed his eyes. He could recite every name on it by memory. Some good men, some bad men, were buried beneath his feet.

What's the matter with you? Naomi's words brought his head up. *The old Charles McIntyre wouldn't have given a nickle about those men and their families. The new Charles McIntyre has turned himself into a whipping boy.*

Someone has to suffer for what happened.

Someone already did.

On a cross.

Charles removed his hat and fanned his face with it, thinking, ruminating. His sins were forgiven. And, as Naomi had so eloquently pointed out, he couldn't pay for the sins of the men who'd died.

He had tried to protect them. He had tried to mitigate the risks, run as safe an operation as possible. But there was always the unforeseen. A man should be ready to meet his maker at any moment.

The catastrophe perpetrated by Delilah was more the fault of a broken, vengeful heart than a lapse in safety standards.

Delilah.

She'd walked away, slithered off into the darkness. Did she have nightmares? Did she feel the loss of these men? The deaths had affected her, but Charles believed Logan's death had rattled her more. A loss from which he doubted she would ever recover.

Part of him hoped she was miserable. Wracked with guilt. Sitting alone in the corner of a dusty saloon fading away.

Suffering as Charles had suffered.

The spiteful thought brought him up short. He had no right to feel this way about her. Jesus had suffered for all this. The sins of murder, pride, selfishness, greed, bitterness. Everything that led to the explosion. Continuing to carry the burden or wish it on Delilah made the cross pointless.

Help me, Lord. I'll do the best I can to let it go. Of all of it.

Charles let his hand fall and straightened up. The offer from MP&G Western Mining Conglomerate rustled in his breast pocket. Decided, he dropped his hat back in place.

The town can be saved, Lord. I don't know about Delilah.

I'm going to be a father. It's time to move past this.

Fourteen

HOPE DISHED a tiny amount of broth to her weak but conscious patient. The woman, whom they had discovered was named Mary Ann, was pale as a cadaver but alive and kicking—well, alive anyway. She could barely hold her eyes open, but after three days of murky consciousness, Hope had to try to get something in her. Fear, however, wiggled in her gut at the unspoken but dire prognosis.

The warm liquid poured into the woman's mouth. Mary Ann closed her eyes and swallowed. Hope breathed a little easier and offered more. Each time she had to touch the patient's lips to get her to take the sip, but soon the small cup was empty.

"That's a start." Hope set the dishware down on the night stand. "Can you tell me how you feel?"

"Like dog vomit," the woman answered unexpectedly in a weak, raspy voice.

"Whoever performed your abortion punctured your uterus. You nearly bled to death."

The woman's eyes fluttered open, a startling green against

the pallor of her skin and bold red hair. "I knew something was wrong. Too much blood."

"You should have come to me straightaway."

"You shoulda done it."

Hope knew what she meant, and the comment was like an ice pick to her heart, pricking her conscience, confusing her moral compass. "I told you, I save lives. I don't take them."

"Lucky for me." She tried to moisten her lips. Hope poured her a glass of water and helped her drink. "Thanks. I don't know what you're so worked up about," she said between sips, her voice growing a little stronger. "I saw it once. It weren't nothing but clumps of blood."

Hope, too, had seen both aborted and miscarried fetuses. Different stages of development. "Though I do not believe in God, Mary Ann, I do think it presumptuous of humans to arbitrarily declare when a clump of blood crosses over to life."

Mary Ann waved a weak hand at her in disgust and pulled away the water. "You don't believe in God but you won't end a pregnancy. You don't make no sense." The woman's body relaxed and Hope could tell she was on the verge of sleeping.

"Mary Ann, can you tell me who performed your procedure?"

"Why?"

Hope thought a noble lie was called for. "Training. I could train her so this doesn't happen again."

"Amanda. How long...how long have I b...?"

"How long have you been here?" The woman nodded. "Three days. You'll be several more recuperating. And I'd suggest you take a few months away from your vocation, if you don't retire altogether."

Mary Ann snorted sleepily. "Too long." She drifted off. "Too long to be away."

~

Amanda swaggered into the Crystal Chandelier, rewarding the hungry stares of patrons with her own inviting glances. A pretty negro girl, Matthew thought, but her vocation was showing on her. Wearing a low-cut gown, Amanda didn't exactly glow; her caramel skin was, in fact, a little dull; her eyes didn't glitter with life, only reflected a weary soul. Weariness that she masked with anger or bravado, whichever suited the occasion.

She spotted him at the bar and made her way toward him with a determined stride. Curious, he laid aside the latest fine from Ian—this one for violating the town's gambling laws. So far, he'd paid one thousand dollars in fines. If the MP&G deal didn't come through or business didn't pick up fast—well, there were no *ifs*. Something had to happen.

He wasn't going to pay this town another red cent.

Amanda was one of the few soiled doves he had working who hadn't been caught yet. Beckwith was a bloodhound, though. Probably wouldn't take him much longer. Maybe such was the reason for her visit.

"Afternoon, Amanda," he said as she approached. "What brings you around before sundown?"

"I ain't your madam, so you could say I'm here as a favor. Thought you might like to know about Mary Ann."

It took him a moment. The older, prickly redhead? "What about Mary Ann?"

"She nearly died. I would have bet against her living, but the new nurse in town got to her. So, she ain't dead. Yet. I hear the jury is still out."

Matthew didn't quite follow this disjointed tale. "What happened to her? Where is she?"

"She tried to get rid of her baby and it didn't go well. She nearly bled to death, but this nurse has her now and is watching over her. Mary Ann might make it."

Matthew considered the news. Mary Ann was popular because she was greedy. She rarely turned away a man because it was late, she was tired, or even had her monthly. He wondered how long she would be down.

"You don't mind me sayin' so, Mr. Miller, you either need to manage your girls more closely or get yourself a madam."

"I don't need any help managing women."

"A good madam knows things. How to keep the girls in line, get 'em turning more money, where to go to get rid of a baby. What to do after. You know any of that?"

Matthew scratched his neck. "Maybe not as much as I should. I made my money in lumber. Whores were recreation."

"You should get a madam then. And I'll tell you something else."

"Well, you're just full of advice today."

The girl glanced at the fine laying on the bar. "I worked for a house over in Omaha. The town fathers tried to shut us down, too. Hit us with fines and violations. Made up vice laws just to confound us. You know what the owner did?"

"No, but I bet you're going to tell me."

"She moved. The whole operation. Outside the city limits. Five feet over the line."

Matthew raised his head, intrigued by the suggestion. "That isn't practical for me. I can't move the Crystal Chandelier. I've got too much in this building."

"Tents are cheap. Besides, what have you paid in fines so far?" She held Matthews' stare for a moment, then shrugged. "Happy to help if I can."

With that, she drifted off through the slim crowd of attentive men, nodding, smiling, swinging her hips, stirring up business for the night. At the bat wings, she glanced back at Matthew—a smug grin on her lips—and pushed out into the sunlight, the fall breeze swirling a handful of leaves into the saloon.

Well, the gal had given Matthew a few things to think about. Did he really have time for wrangling soiled doves anyway? He did have more important fish to fry and the bigger plan was beginning to absorb more and more of his time. Just getting Sally to slap ol' Charles across the snout at church had taken a day of conversation and two double eagles. But the word was she had pulled off the attack with gut-wrenching perfection.

The thought lifted his spirits and he pondered having one of his girls come by for a visit. After all, a benefit of this setup was a little *personal recreation* any time he felt like it. Only, ever since he'd heard about Naomi being with child he had not been availing himself.

He felt differently now. Focused. Determined. Like things were on the verge of changing—in his favor. Amanda and her big ideas were inspiring.

He grinned.

In more ways than one.

Two days later Matthew finally admitted Amanda was on to something. When he found himself hunched over in a sagging, dirty tent, two screaming, cursing, writhing soiled doves snared in the crook of each arm, he decided he'd had enough. He was no nanny. He had better things to do than settle petty squabbles.

"I know you went through my drawers," one girl snarled.

"I ain't been in your tent," the other snapped back.

"I smelled your cheap perfume!"

"Stop it right now," Mathew's voice boomed.

The girls ignored him and continued squirming, twisting, striking out, intent on sinking their nails into each other. They were tiny compared to his massive girth and holding them was easy but tedious.

Fine. His patience gone, he squeezed until the fight went out of both of them and they clawed helplessly at his arms. Then he held on a little longer till they lost consciousness. Reflecting on how golden the silence was, he dropped them to the dirt floor like rag dolls.

He sliced the air with his hands, divorcing himself of the mess and swore, *I am not doing this again*. He flung the tent flap back and stormed onto the dusty, rutted path that wound through Tent Town.

"Amanda!" He bellowed. Hers was the last tent in the row of six and he stomped toward her abode, a few passing miners watching with curious stares. "Amanda!"

Before he reached her threshold, she stepped out to meet him, followed by a blue-gray cloud of smoke and the sweet smell of opium. That brought him up short. "I thought you quit that."

"Oh, I did." A sound came from the tent and a moment later Will Boggess appeared beside her, his dull brown eyes droopy, dreamy. Amanda shoved him back into her tent. "Sleep it off, Will." She grabbed Matthew's arm and pulled him away from her home. "Let's you and me take a walk."

Matthew was not averse to the idea and let the girl lead him. She was half-dressed, wearing only a low-cut shift, corset, and petticoat. He saw the goose flesh rise on her arms and peeled off his blanket coat. "Here."

She slipped into it, all but disappearing inside the huge girth of it. "You here about my idea?"

"Yep."

She pulled the coat tighter. "Then here's my offer. Move all these tents outside the town limits. Promise to build me a cabin, and I'll manage your girls for twenty-five percent."

"Twenty-five percent?" She was crazy. "I'm not giving you that much of a cut."

"Whatever these girls are bringing in now, I can double it. That'd be worth your while. You wouldn't fuss over twenty-five percent then."

Matthew's irritation was simmering. He began to suspect Amanda was still smoking opium. "How do you propose to double what these girls are doing? Sounds pretty pie-in-the-sky to me."

"How often you come down here to check on them?"

"Once a week. Sometimes twice."

"Exactly. You don't stay on top of 'em. They sleep till three or four in the afternoon. Don't start taking customers till dark. Don't take customers after one or two in the morning, if the notion strikes. They need a task master."

"And you've got experience with that?"

The subtle lines in her face hardened. "Oh, yes."

Matthew rubbed his neck, thinking things over. "Move the tents, huh?"

"You had any sense, you'd open another saloon outside the city limits, too."

She'd pointed out that tents were cheap. He'd been pondering her wise but arrogantly delivered advice ever since they'd talked. "All right." He stopped walking. "I'll move the tents. You manage the girls. But first I've got to find a place."

A sly, all-knowing grin twitched on her dark pink lips. "Kentucky Jack is letting his three claims go. Says they're played out. They're side-by-side and plenty big enough for everything we want to do."

Matthew almost chuckled but bit it back. Amanda was hungry. A hungry madam was apt to bite the hand that fed her. Screams like banshees at war erupted from the tent where he'd left the gals on the floor and he made up his mind. "Well, I'll get by there and talk to him. In the meantime..." He gestured grandly, bowing and sweeping his arm in the direction of the feuding women. "They're all yours..."

Matthew left Amanda to deal with the squabbling hens and nearly jogged back to the Chandelier, his mood now was so light. Something told him he'd made the right choice hiring Amanda and he felt like a kid who'd managed to steal candy from the dry goods store. Moving the girls and maybe opening a rowdier saloon just outside the town limits would toss a monkey wrench into McIntyre's and Donoghue's plan to close him down. Child's play, however, compared to what he'd like to do McIntyre...and Naomi.

As he approached the Chandelier, a freckle-faced boy in a Western Union cap saw him coming and ran up to him. "Got this for you, Mr. Miller.'

Matthew backed up a step and glanced at the yellow envelope. A telegram. He fished some change out of his pocket and exchanged it with the boy for the notice.

Well, this could be the door to a fortune or one slamming in my face. He swiped a hand over his lips. "Here goes nothing..." Heart pounding, he snatched the telegram out, tossing the envelope to the wind.

Two words greeted him: OFFER ACCEPTED.

He smacked the note against his palm in victory and slid his gaze up the busy path that led to Defiance's Main Street. Laughing, he nearly kicked his heels together on his way into the Crystal Chandelier. Oh, the things he had to plan. The people he had to hire.

The lives he had to destroy.

If idle hands are the devil's playground, Naomi, just wait till you see what he does with willing hands...

Fifteen

AS CHARLES STRODE down Water Street, the main thoroughfare in Tent Town, he was taken aback by the decline in the area. There were fewer people on the road; the tents had weathered noticeably since his last trip here. More weeds than he remembered grew along some of the less traveled paths. The denizens stirring about were bleary-eyed and slow moving. The strong scents of opium, bacon, and wood fires hung in the chilly air.

The mine closing and the creek playing out was killing Defiance and the rot had started in this quarter. Very little gold, less work. No urgent reason to get out of bed.

Well, Lord, mining might kill them, but so will opium and hopelessness. We'll get this town moving again.

The goal was the only thing giving him the humility to seek out Matthew and offer the man a deal. The idea turned his stomach, but it could rid Defiance of a pestilence and put a lumberyard in Charles' hand. If Matthew was hard up enough for money, he might say yes.

And leave Defiance.

Convinced this course of action was the right one, he strode on toward Matthew's home, the Crystal Chandelier.

Without its raunchy shows and rowdy crowds, the saloon and theater was a ghost of itself. Thumbs tucked in his vest pockets, Charles stood at the doors, peering over them at a meager noon rush. The piano rested silently in the corner, the muttering voices of men enjoying liquid lunches the only sound in the smoky air. He pushed in and scanned the room but did not see Matthew.

"Something I can help you with, McIntyre?" A velvety, baritone voice asked.

Charles cut his eyes to the left. Otis looked up at him from a grouping of chairs he was in the process of painting. Charles liked the mountain of a man much better engaged in such peaceable pursuits. He hoped it stayed that way.

Letting the doors swing shut behind him, he said, "I've come to see Matthew. Is he around?"

Otis laid his brush down across a bucket of paint and rose like a behemoth stirring to life. "He's upstairs." His wide, ebony face hardened with disdain. "I'll see if he's available."

In other words, would he deign to meet with his rival? Charles tried not to take offense. He was in the enemy camp now. Matthew had tried to steal Naomi, and then let an Indian take a clear shot at Charles' back. There was no love lost between the two men, to say the least.

Matthew had hung on in Defiance longer than Charles had expected, but he knew the man was struggling financially. Perhaps today he could drive the final nail in the coffin.

He sensed a glare and looked up. Mathew watched him from the top of the stairs, the heat of his gaze almost a physical slap. Taller even than Otis, wider in the shoulders, but light in every way the Haitian was dark, Matthew leaned into his employee and whispered something. Otis nodded, sauntered down the steps and slipped behind the bar.

Matthew ambled down after a moment and waved McIntyre over. They met at the mahogany as Otis slipped a bottle and two glasses between them. "What brings you to my humble establishment, McIntyre?"

Tension sizzled between them as their eyes, at about the same height, locked, though Matthew was almost as wide in the shoulders as Charles was tall. The two men had not spoken since Matthew's arrival in town, when Charles had warned him about the newly passed Red Light Abatement Laws.

Thus far, the fines had not chased Matthew out of town. Maybe money would nudge him. "I've come to make you an offer for your lumberyard and saloon. I'll buy them both."

Matthew's icy, hazel eyes widened and he turned to the bar. "Well, now." He poured himself a shot, offered the bottle to Charles who waved it away. Matthew capped it, picked up his own drink, swirled the liquor. Charles clamped his jaw, intent on not showing any impatience over this game.

Finally, Matthew tossed back the drink and set down the glass with a loud clink. "They're not for sale."

"You haven't heard my offer."

"Wouldn't change anything."

Charles shifted, resting his back and elbows on the bar so he could survey the crowd. *Crowd* being a generous description. "How much longer can you hold on? Beckwith wants to raid your cribs, arrest your girls. We can keep coming at you. Pass more public nuisance laws."

Matthew poured himself another shot. A slow grin lifted his lips and Charles knew something was going on here he didn't comprehend. "I hear you're selling the mine."

He couldn't even begin to imagine how Matthew had come by that bit of information, but he held his best poker face. *How* didn't matter. The *what* did. What did Matthew think he was going to get out of holding this information? Charles would argue nothing of value.

"What I do with the Sunnyside won't affect you. We're going to legislate you out of Defiance. Go with some money in your pocket or not. It's up to you. But you will go."

"But why would you want to buy my lumberyard?" Matthew mused, ignoring the threat. "Oh," he snapped his fingers. "You need a sawmill for all that lumber you're bringing off the mountain for your spur line."

Charles scratched his bearded jaw to hide his shock. Matthew had entirely too much information about his business. The intelligence could have only come from a few sources. Namely, his railroad contacts. He would find and plug the leak. Later. Right now, he had to reestablish the upper hand with Matthew.

"It would have made things easier for me to buy your lumberyard and go from there. A little faster, but no matter." He lifted a brow in victory. "I'll build my own. Which will further impact your bottom line. Remember, I did offer."

The troubling smirk did not leave Matthew's face. "Yes, yes you did."

~

Would the bad news ever stop coming when it came to Amanda?

Depressed, Hannah set down the fresh sheets at the foot of Mary Ann's bed and nearly sighed aloud.

Hope, about to examine their patient, looked up. "I can see by your face you recognize the name." She pulled the stethoscope from around her neck and straightened. "You know the woman who did this to her?"

Hannah nodded. So much potential. Such a shame. "She used to be one of Charles' Flowers back when the Iron Horse was open. She left for a while, came back, and when she did, he offered to send her to school rather than see her go back into that work."

"My, that was magnanimous of him. What did she want to do?"

"Be a teacher. She said. Charles was going to set up a scholarship for her, pay her way. She walked away from it." Hope didn't say anything and Hannah figured, like all of them, Amanda's actions left her speechless. "She had an opium addiction," she continued. "Emilio and Mollie tried to help her through it, but she won't leave her current vocation."

Hope gripped the stethoscope, her knuckles turning white. With a sigh, she dragged a hand over her hair, poked absently at her bun. "Apparently she's attempting to add new skills to her bag."

"Abortion?"

"Yes. Her ignorance and lack of experience is clear. It's a wonder Mary Ann is still with us."

"Because you have the skills." A troubling thought bubbled up in Hannah. "Do you think Amanda is going to keep providing this service?"

"You know her better than I, what do you think?"

Hannah couldn't tell if the question was rhetorical. Nonetheless, she pondered her few run-ins with Amanda, mulled over the comments Mollie had made about her. "I think she will, yes. She strikes me as greedy. As someone who wants money and power now, anyway she can round it up."

"Then I will go see the marshal about her. If a woman dies from another botched abortion, I won't be able to live with myself. She has to be stopped."

"I know Marshal Beckwith well. I'll go with you, if you'd like."

"That's probably wise. The both of us voicing our concerns may spur him to action."

~

"Not a thing I can do." The marshal reached for a cold cigar sitting in the ash tray on his desk. His bony face, usually hard, intimidating, softened as he lit the stogie. "Dang shame."

"Nothing?" Hope said, taking an incredulous step back from his desk.

He blew smoke heavenward for a moment, and the ladies gave him time to answer, but Hannah was antsy. She sat down on the edge of the seat in front of his desk. "I don't believe that."

"The town has been incorporated. Ian is the acting mayor. I'm duly sworn. Inside those lines," he pointed lazily to a map of Defiance hanging on his wall behind him, "I'm the law. Outside of them, I don't have any jurisdiction."

"Well...well," Hannah sputtered. "We can pass more laws. We can—"

"Won't change anything. Miller has pulled a fast one on us."

"What do you mean?" Hannah asked.

Marshal Beckwith leaned back and rested a foot across his knee. "He moved his operation. Outside Defiance's limits by about thirty feet."

"What?" Hope folded her arms over her chest angrily.

"Yep, he told me straight up he wasn't going to close his saloon or stop running girls. But he would leave town. Now I know he was laughing at me when he said it."

"Move them. He just moved them?" Hannah couldn't believe the man she used to call *uncle* had turned into such a lying, deceitful, manipulative monster. What had happened to his soul?

"Marshal—" Hope started, worked her lips silently for a moment and finally managed, "can you give us any encouragement? Any advice?"

"Yeah, get her to break the law inside the limits."

Hannah hung her head. There had to be something they could—

"What if Mary Ann pressed charges?" Hope asked softly.

"Who's Mary Ann?"

"My patient. The reason we're here. The one this Amanda nearly killed."

"If the crime happened inside the town limits and if she'll press charges, I'll arrest Amanda and get her bail set high as I can. Sounds to me like this is a couple of big ifs."

Hope sighed. "Yes, it is. But I'll try. Amanda is a butcher. One of these girls is going to die if we don't stop her. So, I have to do something."

Hannah agreed with all that, but couldn't shake the feeling Hope was warring with just what the *something* should be.

A Look At: Destiny in Defiance

A shattered past. A town reborn from chaos. A destiny defied by fate... Can love and faith conquer even the darkest secrets?

Charles McIntyre buried his haunted history long ago, emerging as a devoted husband and a man of God with a bold vision for Defiance—a once lawless town poised for transformation. Determined to usher in an era of prosperity and grace, Charles now faces an old nemesis whose return threatens to unravel everything he holds dear. With his family's safety on the line, he must decide: will he lean on the Lord's strength, or will the demons of his past break his resolve?

Riding into Defiance with fierce ambition, Hope Clark is set on proving that a woman's healing touch is every bit as powerful as a man's. But to win the respect she deserves, she must hide her true medical expertise—until lies force her into a heart-wrenching battle between life and death, love and loneliness. Can her hidden truths ultimately lead to redemption, or will they cost her everything?

In a town where every soul is written in defiance, two hearts must confront their inner demons to protect all they cherish.

Order your copy today and discover a stirring tale of courage, faith, and the relentless fight for a brighter future.

AVAILABLE APRIL 2025

About the Author

Heather Blanton is a *USA Today* bestselling author of thirty Christian Western romances, including the highly rated and awarded Romance in the Rockies series. She is also an award-winning script writer. Her Romance in the Rockies series has been optioned for a limited TV series, and her script *Unbridled Hearts* is currently optioned as well.

She grew up in the mountains of Western North Carolina on a steady diet of *Bonanza, Gunsmoke,* and John Wayne Westerns. Her daddy taught her to shoot when she was five, and she can hit that at which she aims.

Her novels are all Christian Western romance because she enjoys creating feisty pioneer women who struggle to find love and hold on to their faith. Like all good, old-fashioned Westerns, there is always justice, a moral message, American values, lots of high adventure, unexpected plot twists, and often a touch of suspense.

www.authorheatherblanton.com